MW00365943

Wish You Were Here

Wish You Were Here

DAVID LELAND

faber and faber
LONDON · BOSTON

First published in 1988
by Faber and Faber Limited
3 Queen Square London WC1N 3AU

Photoset and Printed in Great Britain by
Redwood Burn Limited, Trowbridge, Wiltshire

British Library Cataloguing in Publication Data

Leland, David
Wish you were here.
I. Title
822'.914   PR6062.E46/

ISBN 0-571-15184-1

Dedicated to Laura Daily who died in a road
accident, 28 June 1987, aged fifteen years.

When it comes to writing about film-making, different journalists often ask the same questions: What is your film about? Why did you write this film? Where did the idea begin? etc. I have never found these questions easy to answer.

Half-way through the *Wish You Were Here* promotional tour of the USA in the summer of '87 a journalist told me that, when giving press interviews, Rainer Werner Fassbinder, the German film director and writer, always gave a different answer to the same question – he never repeated himself. My own technique is slightly different: I often give similar answers to the same questions, but each time I try to rethink the answer as if I had never been asked the question – all this in the hope that I might come up with something new and different, that I might come close to the truth.

However, the more I talked the more I realized that hindsight often creates neat and convenient reasons for deeply obscure motives. The reasons given to explain a broken marriage are very different from those that created it. And the same holds true for the making of films and the writing of screenplays. I have great sympathy for the Fassbinder approach; with repetition we all fall into the terrible trap of believing what we have said.

Without doubt, I wrote *Wish You Were Here* more or less by accident. That I do know. At the time I was attempting to write *Personal Services*, a film which was a little more than inspired by the charitable works of Cynthia Payne, she of the Luncheon Voucher Brothel Scandals, a life turned to legend in the courtrooms of England.

The end credits of *Wish You Were Here* show an acknowledgement to Cynthia Payne and Paul Bailey, her biographer, and those who know Paul Bailey's book will be aware that there are incidents and details in the film which correspond to the facts in the book. Those looking for a neat solution to *Wish You Were Here* need look no further. But it was never my intention that

Wish You Were Here should be seen as a prequel to *Personal Services*, that is, about the early life of Cynthia Payne.

Personal Services is everything I experienced in the good company of Cynthia Payne. It is my portrait of her world. But all I did with *Wish You Were Here* was to plunder freely incidents and details in order to fit them into a theme which began much closer to home. The common link I share with Cynthia is that we both grew up in a small, enclosed community. Her stories of her childhood reminded me of my own.

But Cynthia was only one of several women I talked to who had been teenagers during the late forties and early fifties. Some of these women related very painful experiences with tremendous humour, and some talked of incidents which had remained secret for many years. All I had to do was listen.

Family photograph albums also played a part. I don't exactly hate family photograph albums but they do leave me with a creeping feeling of melancholy, particularly my own family photographs. For some people they represent images of the past they have lost – the good old days – whereas to me they are images of a past I have constantly tried to escape.

By looking at the photographs in the albums, it was sometimes easy to recognize the child or the teenager seen in the photographs as the now middle-aged women. The smile and the spark were the same. Whereas with others it was difficult to relate the photographic image of the child to the adult sitting beside me. What had happened to change these people? Why had some transformed so dramatically and others remained the same? What had happened to knock the spark out of the child as she grew into a woman? What does it take to knock the spirit out of us? How does the spirit survive?

As I looked at these images from the past, I looked at young people in the present, including my own daughters, and wondered just how much or little things had changed.

So the film is not intended as a piece of period nostalgia. In part, it was written as a reaction against those films which show the fifties as a carefree romantic era. In reality, the fifties was a period of mounting materialistic aspiration and, at the same time, emotional and sexual repression. Just like the eighties.

Very little has changed in this respect. Then and now, in matters sexual and affairs of the heart, all that the vast majority of young people have to guide them is the ignorance and prejudice of successive generations. And silence.

The British people's deep-rooted sense of respectability is as repressive as ever and we continue to be divided, ruled and isolated by our obedience to class. Future prospects look bleak. I see no champions of (emotional or sexual) enlightenment and tolerance among the pack of born-again moralists who govern us today and hold political power in this country. Where do we go from here?

These are some of the reasons that, in hindsight, I can find for writing *Wish You Were Here* and, having repeated them on numerous occasions, I can now almost believe them. At the time it all felt very different and the results of that process are all in the film and the film is the best explanation I can offer. Perhaps this is why some film-makers never give interviews.

In America, I met a woman who said that *Wish You Were Here* reminded her of all the experiences she had been trying for years to forget. This made her laugh, just like the women I had talked to when writing the screenplay. She was extremely amused by her own reaction.

And in France I sat with five French journalists who discussed what the film meant to them personally. They asked very few questions. Free of the responsibility of having to provide answers, I joined in their discussion and was able to react and talk about the film as just another observer. I think this is the best experience that any film-maker can hope for.

David Leland
August, 1987

Wish You Were Here opened at the Odeon Haymarket, London, on 4 December 1987. The cast was as follows:

LYNDA	Emily Lloyd
ERIC	Tom Bell
DAVE	Jesse Birdsall
HARRY FIGGIS	Geoffrey Durham
AUNT MILLIE	Pat Heywood
HUBERT	Geoffrey Hutchings
TAP DANCING LADY	Trudy Cavanagh
MRS PARFITT	Clare Clifford
VALERIE	Barbara Durkin
GILLIAN	Charlotte Barker
MARGARET	Chloë Leland
LYNDA (aged 11)	Charlotte Ball
MARGARET (aged 7)	Abigail Leland
LYNDA'S MOTHER	Susan Skipper
JOAN FIGGIS	Sheila Kelley
CINEMA MANAGER	Neville Smith
LADY WITH HURT KNEE	Marjorie Sudell
BRIAN	Lee Whitlock
PASSENGER WITH BROLLY	Frederick Hall
MENTAL PATIENT	Bob Flag
DR HILROYD	Heathcote Williams
UNCLE BRIAN	William Lawford
MRS HARTLEY	Pamela Duncan
FISH AND CHIP	
VAN CUSTOMER	David Hatton
POLICEMAN	Ben Daniels
MAISIE MATHEWS	Val McLane
VICKIE	Kim McDermott
CAFÉ MANAGER	Barrie Houghton
COOK	Jim Dowdall
THE BABY	Danielle Phelps
MITCH THE DOG	George

Director	David Leland
Producer	Sarah Radclyffe
Photography	Ian Wilson
Editor	George Akers
Design	Caroline Amies
Costumes	Shuna Harwood
Music	Stanley Myers

Fade up on:
A photograph. 1945. An eleven-year-old girl sits on the kerbstone by the side of the road. She is wearing a Mickey Mouse gas mask. This is LYNDA.
Music and vocal: original recording, the all-time hit of 1945, 'Lost in a Dream'.

1 EXT. SEAFRONT. DAY
1951. A small seaside town. The sea. The waves roll towards the shore. The sound of tap-dancing as 'Lost in a Dream' continues. Credits over.

Camera moves slowly round, the pier comes into view, pan along the pier to the deserted promenade. A lone cyclist pedals her way towards the camera. LYNDA. *She is not yet seventeen. Her dress flies up over*

her knees as it catches in the wind. *Closer and closer . . . The camera pans with* LYNDA *as she cycles past revealing the* DANCER. *On a small painted box, a rather large elderly lady tap-dances and mimes to 'Lost in a Dream'. The music comes from a small wind-up box gramophone. The* DANCER *finishes the song and dance routine with something of a flourish. No applause. No audience.*
End of credits

2   INT.   COLLEGE.   DAY
MRS PARFITT, *the supervisor, watches over a line of* TRAINEE HAIRDRESSERS. *An industrious scene. Each* TRAINEE *has a* VOLUNTEER MODEL *on whom they practise their skills.* LYNDA *is placing curlers into the hair of* VALERIE, *a volunteer model.* LYNDA *is angry. She pays little attention to what she is doing.* VALERIE *is very pretty. She is making eyes at* PETER, *one of the very few male trainees.* PETER *turns on his best smile for* VALERIE. *As* LYNDA *fancies* PETER, *she is very jealous.*

2

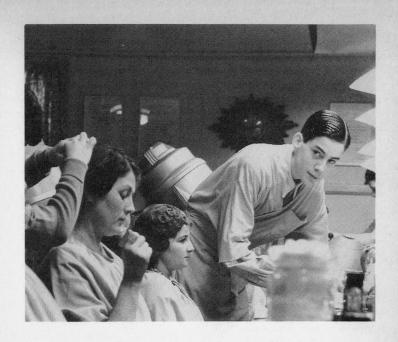

3 INT. HAIRDRESSER'S. DAY
HUBERT MANSELL *is* LYNDA's *father. He is forty-eight. He runs a
small hairdresser/tobacconist's shop in the high street, close to the sea.
Outside, written on the window,* 'HAIRDRESSER MANSELL'S
TOBACCONIST'. *Lettering on the first-floor window above reads:*
'PERMANENT WAVING, *a mini saloon for ladies, open Mon. Wed.
and Fri'.*

HUBERT *wields the electric clippers across the back of a*
CUSTOMER's *neck. The* CUSTOMER *reads the* Sporting Life.
Reg Dixon on the radio.

4 INT. COLLEGE. DAY
LYNDA *tugs at* VALERIE's *hair as, one by one, she puts in the
curlers.* VALERIE *feels the pain.*
VALERIE: Ouch . . . ow!
LYNDA: Keep still.

3

VALERIE: Look, do you mind? You're hurting.
LYNDA: It's all part of the training, none of us is bloody perfect.
(*All the other* TRAINEES *now have their* MODELS *under the dryer and are leaving for a teabreak.* PETER *smiles and winks at* VALERIE *as he walks off.* LYNDA *grabs a dryer and wheels it over to* VALERIE.)
Get your head in there, come on, get a bloody move on.
VALERIE: I say, steady on.
LYNDA: And don't fidget.
(LYNDA *places the dryer over* VALERIE'*s head.*)
VALERIE: Shouldn't I have a hairnet?
LYNDA: Of course not, it doesn't matter.
(LYNDA *turns on the dryer, it roars like a Stuka.*)
There. (*Smiles.*) You always had small tits and a big bum?
VALERIE: (*Can't hear above the din.*) Sorry?
LYNDA: Thought so. I've put you on gas mark 4, back in two days, all right?
(LYNDA *walks off in the same direction as* PETER.)
VALERIE: Can I have a magazine?

5 INT. COLLEGE CANTEEN. DAY
LYNDA *gets a cup of tea from the hatch, served by the* TEA LADY.
LYNDA *is standing with another trainee,* GILLIAN. GILLIAN *has few friends.* LYNDA *watches, eyes fixed on* PETER *who is a few steps away, drinking tea with five other girls.*
GILLIAN: And you can have two skippers in the same rope together, standing side by side – if you know anything about skipping you'll know that this is quite fascinating – you stand side by side and place your near arm round your partner's waist. I do this with my friend Doris. Or you can hold inside hands. We do that too. The swing of the rope must be from the wrist in both cases otherwise the rope will not turn evenly –
LYNDA: – and you fall on your arsehole.
GILLIAN: Yes, well, that's right. And you can have formation skipping teams of any number, would you like to join?
LYNDA: Have I got nice tits or have I not got nice tits?
GILLIAN: Pardon?

4

LYNDA: I got better tits than her. At least I don't wear bloody
    falsies.
    (LYNDA *is left standing alone in the canteen.*)

6   INT.   HAIRDRESSER'S.   DAY
HUBERT *still cutting the same customer's hair. Reg Dixon still on
the radio, pumping away at his organ in the Tower Ballroom,
Blackpool. The customer lowers his* Sporting Life. *This is* ERIC
*(early forties), a thin man, a sharp dresser in an ageing suit, not a
spiv.*
ERIC: Cheveley Wonder. Seven to two.
HUBERT: Ought to go.
ERIC: How much?
    (ERIC *takes out a notebook.*)
HUBERT: A dollar. And cross double it with the other two.

7   INT.   COLLEGE.   DAY
LYNDA *walks quickly down the line of* TRAINEES *and their*
MODELS. *All the* MODELS *(except for* VALERIE*) are now out from
under the dryers.* VALERIE, *under the dryer, no magazine, is looking
hot and uncomfortable.*
LYNDA: I think you're done, dear.
    (LYNDA *turns off the dryer, smoke rises from* VALERIE's *head.*)
VALERIE: It's awfully hot under there.
LYNDA: It's always like that. (*Burns her hand.*) Bugger!
VALERIE: (*Touching her hair*) There's a very unpleasant smell.
LYNDA: (*Smacks* VALERIE's *hand.*) Don't fidget.
    (LYNDA *takes the curlers out of* VALERIE's *hair.*)
VALERIE: You didn't leave me a magazine.
LYNDA: You're getting a free bloody perm, what you expect?
    (LYNDA *gives* VALERIE *a magazine.* MRS PARFITT *walks
    down the line of* MODELS *inspecting the* TRAINEES' *work. The*
    MODELS *look very stylish with their newly permed and waved
    hair. Then she reaches* LYNDA *and* VALERIE. VALERIE's
    *perm is a total disaster, a violent mass of frizzed hair. Suddenly
    aware that she is the centre of attraction,* VALERIE *looks up
    from the magazine and sees the result for the first time.*)
VALERIE: Oh. Oh, no. Oh, no! Look! Look at my hair!

5

(*Becomes hysterical*) Look what you've done to my hair!

LYNDA: I don't know – I think it looks nice. It's nice.

VALERIE: Look at it! Look at it!

LYNDA: Oh, shut up you silly fat cow, you can always wear a hat!

MRS PARFITT: Lynda, come with me.

(VALERIE *sobs as* LYNDA *follows* MRS PARFITT *to her office.*)

LYNDA: (*As she goes*) Balls to the lot of you.

8   EXT.   HAIRDRESSER'S.   DAY

HUBERT *comes out of his shop followed by* LYNDA. *He locks the door. A man walks past with his dog.*

HUBERT: People just don't want to hear a lot of filthy talk when they're having a perm.

LYNDA: I did not swear at her.

HUBERT: It's unprofessional. And disgusting.

LYNDA: I only took it on to please you.

(HUBERT *points up to the first floor where* 'HAIRDRESSING FOR WOMEN – PERMANENT WAVING' *is written on the window.*)

HUBERT: Look, there! Up there, there's an opening. Waiting! All yours. Security for life! This town if full of women crying out for perms.

(MARGARET (*aged thirteen*) *arrives. She is in Girl Guides' uniform and is carrying the troop flag on the end of a pole. It is her job to look after the flag, which she considers to be a serious duty.*)

MARGARET: Hello, Dad.

HUBERT: Hello, Margaret.

(HUBERT *heads for the fish and chip shop, which is next door. The man with the dog is in the chip shop.*)

MARGARET: Hello, Lynda.

LYNDA: Oh . . . bugger off.

HUBERT: (*Flaring up*) Watch your . . . just watch it! Ever since you were a child – you and your disgusting mouth!

LYNDA: Thank you very much.

HUBERT: There's something wrong with you, my girl.

6

LYNDA: I'm bloody bored.
MARGARET: Language.
HUBERT: Cod or haddock, what do you want?
MARGARET: Cod.
LYNDA: Dog.
    (HUBERT *goes into the fish and chip shop.* MARGARET *waits
    at the door.* LYNDA *sits on the kerbstone, looking very bored.*)
A shift in time to –

9   EXT.   THE MANSELLS' HOUSE.   DAY
*1945. Outside the Mansells' house, a reasonably well-maintained
terraced home, close to the sea. The house is modestly festooned with
bunting and a Union Jack.* LYNDA (*aged eleven*) *sits on the
kerbstone. She is wearing a Mickey Mouse gas mask.* AUNT
MILLIE *crosses the road to* LYNDA.
MILLIE: Lynda! Lynda! Look! (*Points up the road.*) There!
    Look! That's your dad!

(*Walking towards the house is Petty Officer* HUBERT
MANSELL *of the Merchant Navy, a large knapsack over his
shoulder.* ELIZABETH MANSELL *and* MARGARET (*aged
eight*) *walk out of the house and wait as* HUBERT *approaches
his home. No great show of excitement and emotion.*)
(*Quietly to* LYNDA) Take that off, Lynda, take it off.
(HUBERT MANSELL *embraces* ELIZABETH, *his wife, watched
by the others, and* LYNDA *still in her gas mask.*)
HUBERT: Millie.
MILLIE: Hello, brother.
(*They kiss each other on the cheek.*)
HUBERT: (*To* MARGARET) Look at you, pretty one, getting
    prettier every day. Have you got a kiss for your father?
    (MARGARET *kisses her father on the cheek. He sees* LYNDA.)
    Is that Lynda?
MILLIE: (*Removes the gas mask.*) Come on, Lynda, take it off.
ELIZABETH: Where's that kiss for your dad, Lynda?
    (LYNDA *kisses her father on the cheek.*)

8

LYNDA: Have you brought us any presents?

10   INT.   THE MANSELLS' HOUSE: FRONT ROOM.   DAY
*The front parlour of the Mansells' home. A celebration is in progress.
Present:* HUBERT MANSELL *(in his Navy uniform);* ELIZABETH
is serving tea to UNCLE HARRY *and* AUNTIE JOAN FIGGIS
(forties) and AUNTIE MILLIE *(late thirties), a widow.* MILLIE *and*
JOAN *are sisters to* HUBERT. LYNDA *and* MARGARET *sit together:
both wear pink dresses, their Sunday best.* HUBERT MANSELL *is
the man to whom his immediate family and relatives look as the man
who made good. Before the war, he worked as a hairdresser on
ocean-going liners (some evidence of this about the place,
photographs, ornaments, etc.) and, although he has spent only short
periods of time at home, he has made good provision for his family.
He is a middle-class man with a lower middle-class background.*
MRS MANSELL, *a gentle, beautiful woman, exists somewhat in his
shadow. A stunned silence. All attention is towards* HUBERT, *except
for* ELIZABETH, *who continues pouring the tea.*
JOAN: No! . . . I don't believe it. When?
HUBERT: This was before the war.
JOAN: I don't believe it.
HARRY FIGGIS: Spectacular.
JOAN: On one of the liners?
HUBERT: That is correct.
JOAN: I just don't believe it, do you?
MILLIE: I don't think the man would lie to us, Joan.
JOAN: No, I mean, I just can't believe it.
HARRY FIGGIS: Neither can I.
MILLIE: I can.
JOAN: You only say that because you never liked her.
MILLIE: Who?
JOAN: You.
MILLIE: Never liked who?
JOAN: Gracie Fields!
MILLIE: I think she screaks.
HARRY FIGGIS: Oh, come on!
    (*General disapproval.*)

9

JOAN: (*To* LYNDA *and* MARGARET) Your father has cut Gracie
    Fields' hair. How about that then?
    (*Only a flicker of reaction from* LYNDA *and* MARGARET.)
HUBERT: (*Correcting* JOAN) Shampoo, set and trim.
JOAN: (*To* LYNDA *and* MARGARET) Shampoo, set and trim.
MILLIE: They've no idea what you're talking about.
JOAN: What?
MILLIE: They think you're off your rocker. (*To* LYNDA *and*
    MARGARET) Don't you?
    (LYNDA *smiles*.)
JOAN: Our Gracie?
HARRY FIGGIS: (*Sings*)
        Sally, Sally, pride of our alley,
        You're more than the whole world
        to me!
JOAN: That's Gracie Fields.
MILLIE: Hardly.
ELIZABETH: I'll get some more water. Show them the picture,
    Hubert.
HUBERT: I was going to. She gave me this.
    (HUBERT *produces a framed photograph of Gracie Fields.*
    Noises of appreciation. LYNDA *whispers something into*
    MARGARET's *ear.*)
JOAN: Oh, look at that.
HARRY FIGGIS: Very nice.
JOAN: I've not seen this before.
MILLIE: Of course not, woman.
JOAN: Can I see what it says?
HUBERT: That's a lock of her hair.
JOAN: It's not.
HUBERT *and* MILLIE: (*Together*) It is.
JOAN: I'm not taking a bit of notice of you, you're just trying to
    get attention. (*Reads*) 'To Hubert, with thanks and good
    wishes, Gracie Fields.'
MARGARET: Lynda just said, 'Up your bum.'
    (*Silence. During the above,* LYNDA *has leaned over and*
    whispered into MARGARET's *ear, 'Pig's willy, up your bum.'*)
    And 'pig's willy'.

10

HUBERT: (*To* LYNDA) Out! Go on – out!
  (HUBERT *ejects* LYNDA *from the parlour.*)
MILLIE: Hubert . . .
HUBERT: Out!
MILLIE: Don't be hard on the girl.

11 INT. THE MANSELLS' HOUSE: HALL. DAY
ELIZABETH *comes out of the kitchen.*
HUBERT: (*To* LYNDA) I've not travelled the oceans of the world
    to come home to language like that. (*Smacks* LYNDA'*s arse.*)
    Bed!
    (LYNDA *walks up the stairs, tears in her eyes.* HUBERT *goes
    back into the living room.*)
ELIZABETH: What's the matter?
Cut to –

12 INT. LYNDA'S BEDROOM. DAY
Late-afternoon sun streams in through the bedroom window. LYNDA
(*aged eleven*) *sits on the bed, facing the window. Tears run down her
cheeks. The camera tracks round to the rear view of her sitting on the
bed, a dark outline against the sun* – *Shifting in time to* –

13 INT. ERIC'S ROOM. DAY
1951. The camera continues to track round the profile of LYNDA
(*aged seventeen*) *sitting on a bed in a large shabby room staring out
of a dirty window into the sunset. Tears run down her face. She is
only partially dressed. Reg Dixon music somewhere in the
background. Sound of door being opened.*
Cut back to –

14 INT. BEDROOM. DAY
1945. LYNDA'*s* MOTHER *walks into the bedroom. She sits with*
LYNDA *on the bed and holds her.* LYNDA *sobs.*
LYNDA: I wish he hadn't come home. I wish he'd stayed at sea
    with bloody Gracie Fields.

15 INT. DOME CINEMA. NIGHT
1951. LYNDA *stands at the exit, torch in hand, watching the film as*

*she waits for the next customer. She is wearing the usherette's
uniform as issued by the Dome Cinema. Two customers, a* YOUNG
MAN *and* YOUNG WOMAN *out on a date, come into the auditorium.*

LYNDA: Tickets. Tickets, please. Where do you think you're
going? Give me your bloody tickets.

(*The* YOUNG MAN *fumbles around for the tickets.* LYNDA
tuts.)

Come on, come on, get in, it's already started. You're
missing the best bit.

(*The* YOUNG MAN *gives* LYNDA *the tickets, she tears them and
leads them into the auditorium, stopping at a row of seats
towards the rear of the cinema.* LYNDA *flashes her torch
towards two empty seats in the centre of the row – disturbing the
activities of courting couples with the searchlight beam of her
torch.* LYNDA *turns towards the screen and is instantly caught
up in the film.* LYNDA *wanders down the auditorium, drawn
towards the screen. She takes a seat, watches the film, lost in
the action. Something of a commotion towards the rear of the
auditorium.* LYNDA *doesn't notice, she goes on watching the
film. The* MANAGER *appears out of the gloom, searching the
cinema for his lone, lost usherette.*)

MANAGER: Lynda . . . Lynda! What are you doing, what do
you think you're doing?

LYNDA: . . . What? Oh.

MANAGER: There's been a terrible accident.

LYNDA: What?

(LYNDA *follows the* MANAGER *back up the auditorium.*)

MANAGER: Mrs Chippenham has fallen and hurt her knee, there
could have been a serious accident.

(*An elderly lady is rubbing her knee, making the most of a
slight knock. She is with her friend, another elderly lady.*)

CUSTOMER: This is just not good enough, you know.

MANAGER: (*Readily agrees.*) It's not.

LYNDA: I was only watching the film.

MANAGER: You're supposed to be the usherette!

(*The* CUSTOMER *moans.*)

CUSTOMER: This is just not good enough.

OTHER CUSTOMER: No, it's not.

(LYNDA *suddenly snaps, thrusts the torch at the two ladies.*)
LYNDA: Here . . . here's the bloody torch, find your own stupid bloody seat!
(LYNDA *strides off towards the exit, removing her Dome Cinema usherette's uniform as she goes. Another lost job opportunity.*)

16   EXT.   BOWLING GREEN.   DAY
Early evening. The local crown green bowling club is out in force. A stately affair, played by elderly gentlemen and watched by octogenarians and limbless ex-servicemen. LYNDA, *on the loose, cycles along the path which runs beside the bowling green close to the seafront.*
GROUNDSMAN: (*As she passes*) No cycling.
LYNDA: Up your bum.
HUBERT: Lynda!
(HUBERT *is playing bowls with* HARRY FIGGIS. LYNDA *stops.* HUBERT *and* HARRY *head in her direction.* LYNDA *becomes aware that she is being watched by* ERIC. *Notebook in hand, he gives a bowler some money and takes money from another bowler, all very casual, but his eye is on* LYNDA.)
Lynda . . . say 'hello' to your Uncle Harry.
LYNDA: Give us a chance.
HARRY FIGGIS: Hello, Lynda.
HUBERT: (*Before* LYNDA *can reply*) Your Uncle Harry –
LYNDA: – Uncle Harry.
HUBERT: – has got a job for you. You start tomorrow.
HARRY FIGGIS: If you want it.
HUBERT: She wants it.
HARRY FIGGIS: Start tomorrow at eight, if that's all right.
HUBERT: You'd better go home to bed.
HARRY FIGGIS: Good. I'll see you at eight, get you started. I'm sure you'll be very happy.
(HUBERT *and* HARRY *head back towards the bowling green.*)
LYNDA: Where? Where do I have to be at eight tomorrow morning?
HARRY FIGGIS: To the garage. The bus company.
(LYNDA *cycles off, aware of* ERIC *who is still watching her. It*

is noticeable that ERIC *walks with a limp.* LYNDA *stands on
the pedals, increases speed so that her skirt flies up, but makes a
point of not looking back. She cycles away from the green and
out on to –*)

17 EXT. SEAFRONT. DAY
Her skirt flying high, LYNDA *rides along the almost deserted
seafront. She cycles past a group of* YOUTHS, *a couple of them in
uniform, who are leaning and sitting on the railings, smoking and
talking. Among the* YOUTHS *is* BRIAN. *The* YOUTHS *nudge*
BRIAN *and wolf-whistle.* LYNDA *cycles on, past a lone figure in a
wheelchair looking out to sea. She stops, gets off her bike, sits on the
railings, her feet and skirt up, and looks out to sea. Distant catcalls
from the* YOUTHS *and, moments later,* BRIAN *(who is very shy)
cycles past.*
LYNDA: Hello.
    (LYNDA *laughs.* BRIAN *does a complete circuit round and back*

14

to LYNDA, *very much aware of his mates, and stops with his cycle tyre against the railings.*)

Hello.

BRIAN: (*Trying not to notice* LYNDA's *legs and knickers*)
Hello.

(LYNDA *laughs.* BRIAN *begins to blush.*)
What you laughing at?

(LYNDA *flaps her skirt around.*)

LYNDA: Phew! Hot. Warm work. Riding bikes.

(LYNDA *laughs again.* BRIAN *looks back at his mates, begins to leave.*)
I fancy you, actually. You can take me to the pictures if you want. There's a Betty Grable film on at the Dome, you can take me if you want.

BRIAN: (*Blushing*) . . . Yeah. Maybe.

LYNDA: Do you think I've got legs like Betty Grable?

BRIAN: . . . I dunno.

(LYNDA *laughs.* BRIAN *begins to cycle away.*)

15

LYNDA: You can take me on Saturday night, I'll buy my own
   ticket.
BRIAN: All right.
   (BRIAN *cycles back to his mates.* LYNDA *stands on the*
   seafront, watching him go.)
LYNDA: (*Calls*) Brian.
   (BRIAN *looks back over his shoulder.* LYNDA *pulls up her skirt*
   and shows her legs.)
   Betty Grable!
   (*The* YOUTHS *cheer and whistle.* BRIAN *begins to wobble,*
   loses his balance and falls off his bike. LYNDA *laughs.*)

18   INT./EXT.   BUS STATION.   DAY
8.35 a.m. LYNDA *walks across a huge bus garage towards an office*
at the end of the garage. Most of the buses are out of the garage, but
some DRIVERS *and* CONDUCTORS *are about to start the second*

16

morning shift. LYNDA *gets a few whistles and a couple of* BUS
DRIVERS *sound the horns on their buses. A* BUS CONDUCTOR
*walks towards her from the opposite end of the garage. He passes
her –*

DAVE: Hello.

> (LYNDA *turns to see* DAVE (*aged twenty-three*). DAVE *is
> extremely handsome and confident.*)

I've not seen you here before.

LYNDA: No.

DAVE: Why not?

LYNDA: I've not been here, have I? Drip.

> (HARRY FIGGIS, *in his inspector's uniform, opens the office
> door.*)

DAVE: Would you like to come dancing with me? The Rex.
Saturday night.

HARRY FIGGIS: Lynda.

17

DAVE: I'm a good dancer.
LYNDA: Can't. Already got a date. Good morning, Mr Figgis.
HARRY FIGGIS: This way, please, you're late.
DAVE: You don't know what you're missing.
LYNDA: Neither do you.

19   INT.   DOME CINEMA: PROJECTION ROOM.   NIGHT
In the projection room, ERIC, *working as the projectionist, changes a reel of film.*

20   INT.   DOME CINEMA.   NIGHT
The Dome Cinema, in darkness and showing the Saturday night main feature: Love Story *starring Stewart Grainger and Margaret Lockwood. The camera tracks along the back two rows occupied, almost exclusively, by courting couples. Some of the boys have their arms round their girlfriends, some are closer, cheek to cheek. In the*

middle of the back row, we find the 'professionals', those who have long since stopped watching the film. Here we find passionate snogging, tongues down throats, hands inside blouses – and perhaps even more. In front of these couples, in the second from back row, near the centre aisle, sit LYNDA and BRIAN. They are watching the film, but LYNDA is itching for some action. BRIAN is a bit slow and hasn't even managed to hold LYNDA's hand or to put his arm round her. He leans over and whispers into her ear.

BRIAN: It's not Betty Grable.

LYNDA: What?

BRIAN: (A bit louder)

It's not Betty Grable. This is not a Betty Grable film . . .

LYNDA: I know! . . . Drip.

(LYNDA sighs, sneaks a look over her shoulder at a couple in the back row. They are kissing. She looks at the screen. They're kissing on screen. BRIAN takes a look at the kissing couple. Very slowly, what seems like hours. BRIAN plucks up courage and slips his arm round LYNDA. LYNDA watches the film, bites *her lip, tries to appear not to have noticed what* BRIAN *is doing.* BRIAN *gets closer to* LYNDA, *almost cheek to cheek. Then, slowly, but very slowly, he moves his hand from* LYNDA's *shoulder down towards her breast (not because he particularly wants to, but more because he thinks this is what he ought to be doing).* LYNDA *is motionless, afraid to move lest she might frighten* BRIAN *and his hand away.* BRIAN's *hand hovers then cups itself, somewhat clinically, over* LYNDA's *breast.* LYNDA *quivers then bursts into tears.*)

BRIAN: What's the matter? . . . Lynda? What's the matter?
　　(*People begin to hush them.* LYNDA *gets up and makes a break for the exit at the back of the auditorium.* BRIAN *follows her.*)

21　INT.　DOME CINEMA: FOYER.　NIGHT
BRIAN *follows* LYNDA *out of the cinema into the foyer.* LYNDA *is still crying.*
BRIAN: What's the matter?
　　(LYNDA *howls even louder and shakes her head.*)
　　I'm sorry. I didn't mean it. Not really. I'm sorry.
LYNDA: (*Shakes her head.*) No. You silly sod.
BRIAN: What? I don't understand.
　　(*Inside the auditorium the film has ended. 'God Save the King' begins to play. People begin to pour out of the cinema, leaving* LYNDA *and* BRIAN *separated on either side of the box office. The* BOX OFFICE GIRL *puts on some lipstick and leaves.*)
LYNDA: (*Shouts across the stream of people*) I liked it. It was nice. Silly bugger.
　　(*The last customers disappear round the corner of the stairs leaving* LYNDA *and* BRIAN *alone once more.* LYNDA *makes a lunge for* BRIAN, *kissing him passionately, just like the movies.* BRIAN *begins to struggle just as the* MANAGER *appears.*)
MANAGER: (*Shouts*) Now then, now then, we'll have none of that here.
　　(BRIAN *breaks away from* LYNDA.)
BRIAN: (*To* LYNDA) Steady on.
MANAGER: What do you think you're doing? This is a picture palace not a brothel.
BRIAN: I'm sorry, sir, I'm very sorry.

20

MANAGER: I'll be talking to your parents about this.

BRIAN: I'm sorry, sir, I won't do it again.

LYNDA: (*Looks at each of them.*) Oh, sod the pair of you.
   (LYNDA *walks off.*)

MANAGER: I'll be talking to your father.

LYNDA: (*At the exit*) Bloody good luck to you.

MANAGER: Clear off before I kick your arse.

BRIAN: Yes, sir.
   (BRIAN *runs off.*)

22   EXT.   THE BACK LANE BY THE MANSELLS' HOUSE.
     NIGHT

LYNDA *walks away from the camera along the back lane which
leads to the back entrance to her home. She walks in through the
back gate, past the shed, up the garden path towards the back door.*

23   EXT./INT.   BUS DEPOT.   DAY

HARRY FIGGIS (*inspector*) *sits in a small cubicle, similar to a*

21

*telephone box. From his cubicle he can check the departures and
arrivals of the buses at the depot. He is drinking Camp coffee from a
thermos and rolling a cigarette. He is happy in his little world. A*
MAN IN TWEEDS *raps on the cubicle window with his brolly and
waves his pocket watch at* FIGGIS. FIGGIS *is puzzled. The man
points to the bus queues. Once out of the cubicle,* FIGGIS *follows the*
MAN IN TWEEDS. FIGGIS *is stunned to discover that the depot is at
a standstill. There are queues of disgruntled people loaded down with
shopping and sitting on suitcases; there are crying children and
unmanned buses. One bus, its engine ticking over, the driver's door
open, is crammed beyond capacity. Somebody presses the bell, it does
not move, but more people try to climb on to the running board as
they suspect the bus is about to leave. Panic sweeps through the
depot as people run for the bus – any bus.* HARRY FIGGIS *makes an
appeal for calm.*

HARRY FIGGIS: Please ... order ... please form into an
orderly queue ... *An orderly queue.* (*Tries to get on to the
overcrowded bus.*) Ladies and gentlemen ... (*Has to shout.*)
Ladies and gentlemen. I am an official of the Southern
Automated Bus Company – no standing on the upper deck,
please.

PASSENGER: This bus is late!

HARRY FIGGIS: Normal service will be resumed as soon as
possible. Additional services will be laid on if necessary.

PASSENGERS: We're not getting off. I'm stuck. (*Etc.*)

HARRY FIGGIS: This bus will not move until it has the
regulation number of passengers.

PASSENGER: Bugger off!

(*The* MAN IN TWEEDS *pokes* FIGGIS *with his brolly.*)

MAN IN TWEEDS: Follow me.

(*The* MAN IN TWEEDS *leads* FIGGIS *to –*)

24   INT.   BUS GARAGE.   DAY

Outraged PASSENGERS *follow* FIGGIS *into the main garage, across
the large open area towards the iron staircase which leads up to the
other office. The staircase is jammed with* BUS DRIVERS *and* BUS
CONDUCTORS. FIGGIS *has to fight his way to the top, followed by*

*everybody else. The camera hoists up and above the crowd to a point
of view in through the office window. Inside the office,* LYNDA *is
showing her legs to a full house of highly appreciative Southern
Automated Bus Company staff.* DAVE *is in the front row.* LYNDA *is
more than aware of the effect she is creating, but it is being done in
the spirit of good fun. Unlike at the seafront, she is now wearing
high-heeled shoes, nylons, suspenders and camiknickers.*

BUS DRIVER: What about your knickers?

LYNDA: Marks and Spencer's, do you like them?
  (*Of course they do.*)
  Look nice, don't they? And they go right up to my belly
  button. Camiknickers, that's what they're called. Quite
  loose round the leg, can you see?

HARRY FIGGIS: Stop! Stop! Stop this!
  (*Boos and jeers from the staff.*)
  Out! Out! (*To* LYNDA) You're fired.
  (*More boos and jeers.*)
  You're all fired! No!! No, you're not. You're not fired. (*To*
  LYNDA) Just you, you're fired.
  (*Even louder boos and jeers.*)
  You lot – out! Out! Back to the buses. Get back!!

LYNDA: I was only showing them my new knickers, Mr Figgis.
  Look.

25   INT.   MENTAL HOME.   DAY
A corridor in the Holly Park Institute for the Mentally Deranged. A
PATIENT *singing 'Goosey Goosey Gander' is led down the corridor
past* HUBERT MANSELL *who is waiting outside an office. Some
strange noises can be heard in the background.*

26   INT.   HOLROYD'S OFFICE.   DAY
LYNDA *is with* DR ROLAND HOLROYD, *a psychiatrist.* HOLROYD
*dresses with a certain amount of artistic flare and smokes Du
Maurier cigarettes.*

DR HOLROYD: Your father says you have sworn constantly since
  you were a child.

LYNDA: My first word was bum.

DR HOLROYD: . . . Really? He's very worried about your . . .

LYNDA: Swearing.

DR HOLROYD: Yes, that's right, and . . . and your behaviour. As I said, I am here to help you.

LYNDA: That's nice.

DR HOLROYD: Once we discover what kind of help you need. Good. Do you know what a psychiatrist is?

LYNDA: No.

DR HOLROYD: You don't.

LYNDA: Well, yes, I do, but, you know, not really.

DR HOLROYD: Do you swear a lot, Lynda?

LYNDA: I don't know.

DR HOLROYD: Do you resent coming here, do you mind coming to see me?

LYNDA: No, why should I? I thought it would make a nice day out.

DR HOLROYD: The place is jam packed full of loonies.

LYNDA: I know.

DR HOLROYD: Yes. Good.

LYNDA: Haven't done anything yet.

DR HOLROYD: Do you know lots of swear words, Lynda?

LYNDA: A few. What about you?

DR HOLROYD: I'll tell you what we'll do, Lynda – do you mind if I call you Lynda?

LYNDA: I'd prefer that to Beryl.

DR HOLROYD: Is Beryl your second name?

LYNDA: No.

DR HOLROYD: Er . . . I'll tell you what we'll do . . .

LYNDA: Yes.

DR HOLROYD: Let's go through the alphabet, we'll start at A . . .

LYNDA: Best place.

DR HOLROYD: . . . and I want you to tell me all the swear words you know beginning with A, then we'll go on to . . .

LYNDA: B.

DR HOLROYD: . . . and so on, you get the picture?

LYNDA: Yes.

24

DR HOLROYD: Good. So, A. The letter A.

LYNDA: Arse.

DR HOLROYD: Arse. Good.

LYNDA: This is silly. You really want me to do this?

DR HOLROYD: You feel foolish, do you, when you swear?

LYNDA: Only when I'm sat here like this.

DR HOLROYD: Do you feel guilty?

LYNDA: What about?

DR HOLROYD: Let's go on. Arse.

LYNDA: Hole.

DR HOLROYD: Hole?

LYNDA: Arse.

DR HOLROYD: Hole.

LYNDA: That's it.

DR HOLROYD: (*Catching on*) Ah! Good. Yes.

LYNDA: And holes.

DR HOLROYD: Of course. Let's move on to B.

LYNDA: Leave those behind. Ha, ha.

DR HOLROYD: B.

> (LYNDA *begins to sense that* DR HOLROYD *is slightly titillated by this little game.*)

LYNDA: Bloody, bastard, bugger, bum.

DR HOLROYD: Very good.

LYNDA: And holes.

DR HOLROYD: Holes?

LYNDA: Bum.

DR HOLROYD: Holes. Yes, of course. Very good.

> (DR HOLROYD *takes another Du Maurier and lights it.*)
> Now, Lynda . . . C.

LYNDA: We missed balls.

DR HOLROYD: So we did. Never mind. *C*.

LYNDA: (*Knows what he's thinking of.*) No. Can't think of nothing.

DR HOLROYD: Take your time.

LYNDA: (*Pretends to think.*) No.

DR HOLROYD: Think really hard now . . . the letter C . . . something really filthy . . . very, very dirty.

LYNDA: (*Thinks hard*) Ca ca?

25

DR HOLROYD: (*Totally bemused*) . . . ca ca?

LYNDA: Ca ca. Poo poos.

DR HOLROYD: (*Slightly rattled*) Are you feeling ashamed?

LYNDA: What of?

DR HOLROYD: Of what you're really thinking.

LYNDA: I'm not thinking of anything.

DR HOLROYD: Yes, you are.

LYNDA: No, I'm not.

DR HOLROYD: Very well then, *D*

LYNDA: Damn.

DR HOLROYD: Precisely. *F*. The letter F.

LYNDA: You've missed out E.

DR HOLROYD: There isn't one beginning with E.

LYNDA: There might be.

DR HOLROYD: There isn't. Take my word for it.

LYNDA: We could give it a try.

DR HOLROYD: *F*.

LYNDA: F.

DR HOLROYD: F. Can you think of a filthy, dirty, smutty word

26

starting with F? Not too hard I should have thought, Lynda.

LYNDA: (*Shakes her head*.) No.

DR HOLROYD: Oh, come on, come on, of course you can.

LYNDA: No, I can't.

DR HOLROYD: Of course you can. I can. Anybody can.

LYNDA: Well what then? You tell me.

DR HOLROYD: You must be one of the last people on God's earth who doesn't know. Everybody knows a swear word beginning with the letter F.

LYNDA: Then what are you asking me for?

DR HOLROYD: Because I want to hear you say it.

LYNDA: You dirty old bugger.

DR HOLROYD: Beryl –

LYNDA: Lynda.

DR HOLROYD: How do you expect me to help you if you are not prepared to help yourself?

LYNDA: I don't want you to help me. I only came here to please my dad. And because I thought it would make a nice day out.

(DR HOLROYD *takes a final, deep pull on his Du Maurier and stubs it out*.)

27   INT.   MENTAL HOME CORRIDOR.   DAY

The PATIENT, *still singing 'Goosey Goosey Gander', and the* NURSE *make their way back along the corridor from wherever they have been.* LYNDA *waits as* DR HOLROYD *chats quietly to* HUBERT MANSELL.

DR HOLROYD: It is difficult to be sure without further investigations, but I would conjecture that something has most definitely happened to Lynda during the course of her adolescence.

HUBERT: Her mother died when she was eleven, would that have anything to do with it?

DR HOLROYD: Possibly.

HUBERT: What can I do?

(*They become aware that* LYNDA *is trying to hear what they are*

saying. They move away from her down the corridor – their
backs to LYNDA. LYNDA *puts out her tongue, mouths 'Fuck*
off' and wiggles her arse at them.)
I'm ashamed of her, doctor, she's an embarrassment, is
there nothing you can do?

DR HOLROYD: She's a difficult case. Can you make some more
appointments for her?

HUBERT: Will it cost the same for each visit?

DR HOLROYD: Yes, it will.

HUBERT: Then I'm not sure that it's worth it.

(LYNDA *lifts her skirt and shows them her knickers.* HUBERT
and DR HOLROYD *turn and look back at* LYNDA, *who now
stands in the corridor, hands behind her back, smiling sweetly at
the two men.)*

28   INT.   REX BALLROOM.   NIGHT
*Saturday night at the Rex Ballroom. Against a painted backdrop of
the Manhattan skyline, stars and glittering lettering proclaim:* 'HEY
HEY USA!' *The Stan Stacey Dance Orchestra plays out the final*

bars of 'All Aboard the 704'. *Several couples on the dance floor. At one end of the dance hall, away from the entrance, sit those few ladies who have been unfortunate and not been invited to dance. In the distance, at the other end of the hall, near the entrance, stand a legion of males, the shy, the boozers and those with two left feet. The number comes to a swinging end, complete with train whistles and bells. Applause. Some couples separate, some stay together. The camera moves in on* LYNDA, *all smiles as she stands arm in arm with* DAVE, *the bus conductor.*

STAN STACEY: Thank you, thank you. And now ladies and gentlemen, a star number from our feature vocalist, Rudy Stephenson. Especially for all you sweethearts and lovers ... (*looks at a piece of paper*) and for Trevor Wilson and Tessa Phipps who became engaged today...
(*Cheers, rolls on the drums, spotlight picks up first on* LYNDA *and* DAVE *by mistake, then on* TREVOR *and* TESSA. LYNDA *smiles and waves the moment she comes into the spotlight.*)
Thank you. Yes, we hope you will all stick very close together as Rudy gives his own very special rendition of

that all time favourite . . . 'Lost in a Dream'.
(*Lights change, very moody, follow spots, glitter balls, etc.*
RUDY STEPHENSON *sings 'Lost in a Dream'.*)
RUDY STEPHENSON: (*Sings*)
    When it comes to having dreams
    Love has always played the leading part
    I don't play for dimes and nickles
    I don't play to be the last.
    I shoot first, shoot to kill.
    I aim straight for the heart.
Chorus:
    You won't . . . forsake me.
    To heaven . . . you'll take me.
    Don't try . . . to wake me.
    I'm just Lost in a Dream.
(DAVE *is an excellent dancer, handsome and debonair.* LYNDA
*is in seventh heaven as he guides her gently round the dance
floor.* DAVE *whispers something into* LYNDA's *ear, she smiles,*

he kisses her. The camera moves past LYNDA *and* DAVE *and in on the watching, left-out faces of the legion of men at the end of the ballroom. Here, cigarette in mouth, slightly pissed, we find* ERIC. *He watches* LYNDA *as she dances with* DAVE.)

29   EXT.   REX BALLROOM.   NIGHT
Arm in arm, LYNDA *and* DAVE *walk out of the main entrance of the Rex Ballroom. In the background, 'Lost in a Dream' continues.*

30   EXT.   STREET.   NIGHT
Distant strains of 'Lost in a Dream'. LYNDA *and* DAVE *walk along the road and turn into the front gate of a small Victorian/Edwardian house. The house is set back and separated from the road by a garden. They walk along the path to the front door.*

31   INT.   DAVE'S HOUSE: BEDROOM/LANDING.   NIGHT
Point of view across the bed on to the landing. DAVE *and* LYNDA *walk up the stairs and into the bedroom.* DAVE *turns on the light.*
DAVE: This is my grandma's bedroom.
LYNDA: That's your grandma's bed.
DAVE: What did you tell your dad?
LYNDA: I'm staying with my friend, Pauline. Where's your gran?
DAVE: Tunbridge Wells. She's going to leave me this house in her will.

32   EXT.   DAVE'S HOUSE.   NIGHT
The lights are on in the upstairs front bedroom. DAVE *draws the curtains. Standing at the gate, looking towards the house, is* ERIC. *He stands for some moments, drawing on a cigarette, looking up at the bedroom window. Then he walks off, with a slight limp, down the road.*

33   INT.   DAVE'S HOUSE: BEDROOM/LANDING.   NIGHT
Dave's grandmother's bedroom. A large double bed with ornate wooden head and foot. LYNDA, *in her nightdress, sits on the bed, waiting for* DAVE. *She has been waiting for some time. She looks*

31

towards the half-open bedroom door. Still no DAVE. LYNDA *walks
out of the bedroom and looks along the landing towards the
bathroom. The bathroom light shines through the frosted glass of the
bathroom door.* LYNDA *walks to the door and listens.* LYNDA *taps
on the door.*

LYNDA: You all right in there?

DAVE: I'll be out in a minute.

LYNDA: You been in there bloody hours.

DAVE: You get into bed.

LYNDA: (*As she walks away*) I might fall asleep.

34   INT.   DAVE'S HOUSE: BEDROOM.   NIGHT

LYNDA *sits in the large double bed.* DAVE *makes a casual but grand
entrance into the bedroom. He is wearing bright canary-yellow
pyjamas and is smoking a cigarette in a cigarette holder.*

LYNDA: Cor, look at you.

DAVE: (*Leans on the edge of the bed.*) Do you fancy me?

LYNDA: Not half as much as you fancy yourself.
   (DAVE *sits on the edge of the bed and kisses* LYNDA *on the
   cheek, close to the mouth.*)
   What kind of cigarette is that?

DAVE: Du Maurier.

LYNDA: Really?

DAVE: They're the best.
   (DAVE *kisses her again, on the mouth.*)

LYNDA: (*Tastes the kiss.*) Toothpaste.

DAVE: I'm going to make love to you –

LYNDA: I do bloody hope so.

DAVE: – like you've never been made love to before.

LYNDA: Shouldn't be too difficult.

DAVE: I'm going to do it to you – right now.
   (DAVE *gets into bed with* LYNDA.)

LYNDA: (*Sits up in bed.*) Er . . . I might have a baby – just
   thought I'd mention it before we go too far.

DAVE: No. No chance.

LYNDA: I'm not so Dolly Dumb as I look, you know.
   (DAVE *takes a packet of Durex from his pyjama pocket.*)

DAVE: Don't worry, Dave thinks of everything.

LYNDA: Oh – Durex!

DAVE: (*Corrects her pronunciation*) – Durex –

LYNDA: My dad sells these – what are they for?

DAVE: To stop you having babies.

    (LYNDA *opens the packet.*)

LYNDA: What?! Crafty bugger. No wonder he hides them under the counter. (*Looking at a plonker*) Ugh . . . you don't have to eat them, do you?

DAVE: (*Smiles.*) No.

LYNDA: You've been done, there's not one in this packet.

DAVE: That's because I'm wearing it.

LYNDA: Are you?

    (LYNDA, *sensing that it's all about to happen, gets down into the bed with* DAVE.)

DAVE: Yes, I am.

LYNDA: Oh! . . . Oh, so you are.

    (DAVE *kisses* LYNDA.)

    Oh, come on, Dave, quick, let's do it.

DAVE: Hold on.

    (DAVE *plunges forwards, his head sinking into the pillow, and rolls over to one side.*)

    What you laughing at?

LYNDA: I'm not! I'm not! (*Kisses him.*) Come on.

DAVE: Hang on . . . Here.

    (*After a lot of fiddling about and increasingly hysterical giggles from* LYNDA, DAVE *makes contact.*)

LYNDA: Oh!

DAVE: Yes.

    (*Suspended animation, neither of them moves. Their faces are very close. They look into each other's eyes.*)

LYNDA: What do we do now?

    (DAVE *quivers for some moments.*)

DAVE: Oh . . . Lynda . . . any more fares please!

    (DAVE *plunges forwards, his head sinking into the pillow and rolls over to one side.*)

LYNDA: Oh. That was quick.

DAVE: Did you like it?

LYNDA: Oh, it was nice. But quicker than I expected.

DAVE: (*Smiles.*) Don't worry.

LYNDA: Is it always as quick as that?

DAVE: No. Don't worry, you'll soon get the hang of it. We've got all night.

LYNDA: That's good. (*Still holding the Durex*) Then you'd better swallow another one of these.

35 EXT. DAVE'S HOUSE. DAY

Morning. A man and a dog walk through the gateway and up to the front door.

36 INT. DAVE'S HOUSE: BEDROOM. DAY

LYNDA *lies asleep cradled in* DAVE's *arms. The empty contraceptive packets lie on the bedside cabinet. They both wake with a jolt as the man knocks on the front door.*

LYNDA: What's that? Oh, my God, who is it?

    (DAVE *leaps out of bed.*)

DAVE: Blooming heck.

LYNDA: Dave, who is it? It's my Dad.

DAVE: Wait a sec.

LYNDA: (*Panic taking over*) If it's my Dad, tell him I'm not here.

    (*The dog can be heard barking. The man yells 'David!' through the letterbox.*)

DAVE: It's my uncle.

UNCLE BRIAN: (*Shouts*) David! You in there, David?

LYNDA: Oh, my God!

DAVE: I'll have to let him in.

LYNDA: No.

DAVE: Under, quick!

LYNDA: What?

DAVE: Get under the bed.

    (DAVE *hustles* LYNDA *under the bed.*)

    (*Pushing her under the bed*) Quick. He's got a key.

LYNDA: If he's got a key, what's he knocking the bloody door for?

34

UNCLE BRIAN: You up there, David?
> (DAVE *chucks Lynda's clothes under the bed, grabs the empty contraceptive packets and leaps into bed.* UNCLE BRIAN *comes into the bedroom preceded by Mitch, an old and lumbering Jack Russell terrier, who snuffs around the room.*)
> What are you doing in your grandmother's bed?

DAVE: What's it look like?

UNCLE BRIAN: Your grandma know you're sleeping in her bed?

DAVE: Of course she does.

UNCLE BRIAN: She comes back from Tunbridge Wells, finds you in her bed, there'll be trouble.

DAVE: Yeah, all right, so what?
> (*Mitch has sniffed his way under the bed where he has found* LYNDA. *He begins to growl at her.*)

UNCLE BRIAN: Mitch! I'm given to understand you brought a girl home here last night.

DAVE: What?
> (*Mitch begins to bark at* LYNDA. LYNDA *tries to shoo him away.*)

UNCLE BRIAN: Mitch!

DAVE: Who told you that?

UNCLE BRIAN: Never you mind.

DAVE: I went dancing last night.

UNCLE BRIAN: At the Rex.

DAVE: But I didn't bring home any girl, Uncle Brian. Not me.
> (*Mitch's attention has been diverted by something on the floor which he begins to sniff at with considerable canine curiosity. He picks it up in his teeth and walks back to* UNCLE BRIAN. *Mitch sits. From beneath the bed,* LYNDA *sees clearly that hanging from Mitch's mouth is a used contraceptive.*)
> I wouldn't dream of such a thing, Uncle Brian.

UNCLE BRIAN: I should hope not. (*Begins to leave.*) You should be up. This time o' day. Should be out doing something.
> (*Mitch follows* UNCLE BRIAN *out of the room, the contraceptive still hanging from his mouth.*)

DAVE: Where have you been, church?

UNCLE BRIAN: (*From the stairs*) Taking the dog for a walk. Keeping an eye on things.
> (*The front door slams.* LYNDA *crawls from beneath the bed.*)

LYNDA: The bloody dog's got one of your plonkers!

DAVE: I know, I know.

(*They look out of the window. Heading up the road, in the direction of the house, we can hear the local Salvation Army band.* UNCLE BRIAN *and Mitch walk to the front gate and along the road. Mitch is still carrying the contraceptive.* LYNDA *laughs.*)

LYNDA: Look at the bloody thing, look at it!

Cut to —

37 EXT. DAVE'S HOUSE. DAY

Outside the gate, UNCLE BRIAN *stops to put a lead on Mitch. He sees the contraceptive, realizes what it is, hits the dog on the head to make it drop it. He looks towards the camera beyond which (out of vision) the Salvation Army Band can be heard. Without realizing where it has come from,* UNCLE BRIAN *kicks the contraceptive into the gutter. Hold on* UNCLE BRIAN *and Mitch as they walk off down the road escaping from the approaching Salvation Army Band.*

38 EXT. HAIRDRESSER'S. DAY

HUBERT MANSELL *leaves his shop and locks up as usual. He walks off up the road.*

39 INT. THE MANSELLS' HOUSE. DAY

LYNDA *opens the door for* MARGARET. MARGARET, *in her Guide's uniform, tries to manoeuvre the troop flag out into the street.* LYNDA *has been washing her hair, she is wearing a slip and has a towel over her shoulders to cover her bra.*

LYNDA: Oh, come on, for God's sake.

MARGARET: Sorry.

(*As she is about to close the front door, she notices* ERIC. *They stare at each other for a moment.*)

LYNDA: What do you want?

ERIC: Father in?

LYNDA: No.

ERIC: (*Mimics her*) No.

36

LYNDA: Not back yet.

ERIC: (*Mimics her*) Not back yet.

LYNDA: Come in if you want.

ERIC: Can I?

LYNDA: Or stand there like a dummy, I don't care.

　　(LYNDA *turns and walks back up the stairs towards her*
　　bedroom leaving ERIC *on the step. He walks into the house.*)

40　INT.　BUS STATION.　DAY

A bus draws into the garage. DAVE *jumps off the running board of*
the bus as HUBERT MANSELL *walks out of the office with* HARRY
FIGGIS.

HARRY FIGGIS: Dave!

　　(FIGGIS *watches as* HUBERT *walks over to* DAVE. *They meet*
　　in the centre of the garage. HUBERT *talks,* DAVE *listens.*)

41　INT.　THE MANSELLS' LIVING ROOM.　DAY

LYNDA *walks into the living room.* ERIC *is standing at the*
fireplace. LYNDA *is wearing a new skirt and carries a handbag. She*
looks very pretty. ERIC *stares at* LYNDA. LYNDA, *not to be outdone,*
stares back.

LYNDA: I don't know where he is.

ERIC: I didn't say you did.

LYNDA: So what you staring at?

ERIC: You going to take up hairdressing like your dad?

LYNDA: No thanks.

ERIC: Reckon you could give me a trim?

LYNDA: Get the pudding basin. I'll give it a try.

ERIC: So, you're the troublesome one, eh?

LYNDA: What do you mean?

ERIC: (*Mimics her*) What do you mean? That's what your dad
　　calls you. Says you're a troublesome bugger.

LYNDA: Language.

ERIC: Can't wait to get rid of you.

LYNDA: Why are you limping?

ERIC: (*Mimics her*) What do you mean?

LYNDA: You got something the matter with your leg?

ERIC: (*Moves towards* LYNDA.) No. Why? You got something the matter with yours?

LYNDA: (*Smiles.*) Don't think so, no.

ERIC: Think you're it, don't you?

LYNDA: What do you mean?

ERIC: What do you mean?

> (LYNDA *laughs.*)

Troublesome bugger. Think you're God's gift, don't you?

LYNDA: I think I'm all right, thank you very much.

ERIC: I think you're all the same, don't know what you've got it for.

> (ERIC *touches* LYNDA's *knee, just above the hem of her skirt.* LYNDA *reacts but does not pull away.*)

All you young girls, just scared, all talk, scared of a real man, ain't you?

> (*Hold on* LYNDA's *face as* ERIC *runs his hand up the inside of her thigh to the top of her stockings. Then he begins to explore the inside of her knickers.* LYNDA *is both shocked and excited. A frightening and compulsive sensation.*)

LYNDA: You bugger. (*Begins to shake, just a little.*) You dirty bugger.

ERIC: Where's your sister?

LYNDA: Girl Guides. She's gone to the Girl Guides.

> (LYNDA *is getting very turned on. Then the click of the front door jolts them apart. They retreat to opposite sides of the room.*)

ERIC: I'll see you later, out the back, when the pubs shut.

LYNDA: That's what you think.

> (*The front door slams.* HUBERT MANSELL *walks in from the hall.*)

ERIC: Hubert.

HUBERT: Oh, Eric. How did we do?

ERIC: Not so bad, not so bad.

HUBERT (*To* LYNDA) I want a word with you.

LYNDA: I'm going out.

HUBERT: Are you?

> (ERIC *takes out a considerable bundle of banknotes and begins to count notes from off the top.*)

ERIC: Great Eastern, Blue Boy and Tee's Delight. On the nose, cross doubles and a treble. Everyone a winner.

HUBERT: Very nice.

LYNDA: (*Mimics*) Very nice.

ERIC: Sixteen pounds, seven and six.

HUBERT: You're a toff – here.

> (HUBERT *shoves a pound note into* ERIC's *top pocket, a very generous commission.*)

ERIC: Thanks.

HUBERT: Stay for a drink.

ERIC: No, got to push on.

LYNDA: Got to push on.

HUBERT: Come on, parrot –

LYNDA: – parrot –

HUBERT: See the man to the door.

LYNDA: Yes, Dad.

ERIC: (*Moves to the door.*) She's a lovely girl though, Hubert, isn't she?

HUBERT: You think so?

ERIC: Oh, yes, lovely girl.

HUBERT: (*Laughs*) Then make me an offer!

> (*They both laugh.*)

LYNDA: Ha, ha.

HUBERT: (*Repeats his joke.*) Make me an offer! No reasonable offer refused.

> (LYNDA *walks down the hall and opens the front door.*)

ERIC: Half a dollar. On the nose.

> (*They both laugh.*)

HUBERT: Done.

> (HUBERT *stays in the living room.* LYNDA *holds the front door open for* ERIC.)

LYNDA: (*Smiles as he passes.*) Hope your finger stinks.

ERIC: See you later.

LYNDA: Cock off.

> (LYNDA *closes the front door behind* ERIC, *then heads for the kitchen and the back door.*)

42 EXT. THE MANSELLS' HOUSE: BACK GARDEN. DAY

LYNDA *heads down the garden path towards the shed where she collects her bike.* HUBERT *follows her.*

HUBERT: Eh! Where do you think you're going?

LYNDA: Out.

HUBERT: Oh no you're not.

LYNDA: Oh yes I am.

HUBERT: (*Sharp*) You're not, I'm telling you you're not. You stay in for a change.

LYNDA: I stay in, look after boring you know who, you go to the pub. Lovely.

HUBERT: Wrong. Freemasons.

LYNDA: Same thing. Yap, yap, yap, bit of this – (*tippling*) – then on to the club or pub with Long John Silver. It's all bloody boozing.

HUBERT: (*Getting rattled*) Lynda, I don't want to hear it, I won't have this kind of talk! Do you hear? I won't have it. I've had enough of this, I give the orders, I've had enough.

LYNDA: Get rid of me then. Make me an offer. Ha, ha.
(LYNDA *has got her bike out of the back gate.*)

HUBERT: You stay away from bus conductors!
(HUBERT *tries to keep his temper down.* LYNDA *realizes she's been rumbled.*)
Bus conductor! Look at you. That's just about your . . . I'm ashamed to be your father.

LYNDA: Oh . . . Cock off!
(HUBERT's *temper flares, but* LYNDA *is away on her bike before he can get out of the gate.*)

HUBERT: You're not too old, madam, remember that.
(*He watches her go then, still in a black mood, makes his way back up the garden path. He treads on an upturned rake and narrowly avoids getting a blow to the head.*)

43 EXT. DAVE'S HOUSE. DAY
The street in which DAVE *lives with his grandmother.* LYNDA *cycles past the house. No sign of* DAVE. *She turns and cycles back past the house. Still no sign of* DAVE. *She sees* UNCLE BRIAN *and Mitch, the dog, walking towards the house. She watches as they approach*

the front door. The front door opens, UNCLE BRIAN *and Mitch go in, but she cannot see who opened the door. She cycles on, away down the road.*

44   EXT./INT.   THE MANSELLS' HOUSE: BACK GARDEN/
BEDROOM.   NIGHT
Point of view from Lynda's bedroom of the back garden, lawn and shed lit by moonlight. The glow of a cigarette then, standing in the lane at the bottom of the garden, ERIC. *Cig in his mouth, he looks up at Lynda's bedroom, but cannot see* LYNDA *behind the curtains. In the bedroom.* LYNDA *does not move. She stares out of the window at* ERIC.

LYNDA: You'll have to wait a bloody long time, Mr Stinky
    Finger, Parrot Chops, Long John Silver.
    (ERIC *takes the final drag on his cigarette, looks up at Lynda's window, and decides to abandon his vigil. He walks off up the lane.*)

45   EXT.   THE MANSELLS' GARDEN.   NIGHT
The back door opens and LYNDA, *barefoot and wearing her nightgown, tiptoes her way down the garden path. She looks carefully round the corner of the shed and down the lane, being cautious not to be seen by* ERIC. *As* ERIC *disappears from view at the end of the lane, pausing to light another cigarette,* LYNDA *gives him the V sign.*

LYNDA: Up your bum, Mr Long John Silver.
    (*Quietly singing 'up your bum' and humming to herself,* LYNDA *skips and dances around the lawn in the moonlight, sending V signs in the direction of* ERIC, *her sleeping father, sister, the neighbours, everyone. She gets louder as she gets carried away with the dance. She dances from one end of the garden to the other, leaping higher and higher into the air. A neighbour's window flies open.*)

MRS HARTLEY: What's going on down there?!
LYNDA: Trying to find the cat, Mrs Fartley.
    (LYNDA *turns her back on* MRS HARTLEY *and bends over. The back of her nightdress flies up revealing her bare bum.*)
    Puss, puss, puss, puss.
    (MRS HARTLEY *retreats in horror.*)

46   INT./EXT.   A MOBILE FISH AND CHIP VAN.   DAY
*The mobile fish and chip van is parked on the promenade. It's
lunch-time and there's a long queue. Through the customers at the
counter, we see that* LYNDA *is serving the fish and chips. She is
wearing a white coat, apron and white hat, all an edge too large.
She is working hard and fast. She finishes serving one customer.*
LYNDA: Next.
    (*And looks up to serve the next person in line. It is* DAVE. *A
    shock for both of them.* LYNDA *had not expected to see him,*
    DAVE *had no idea that* LYNDA *was working in the fish van.*)
DAVE: Two sixes.
LYNDA: Two sixes.
    (*As* LYNDA *gets two paper bags and starts to fill them with
    chips, her eye wanders from Dave along the promenade to
    where she sees a pretty young woman on a bike. She is holding
    another bike, a gent's racer.*)
    Open or closed?
DAVE: Open, please.
LYNDA: Two sixes. A shilling, please.
    (DAVE *places the money on the counter: a threepenny piece, six
    pennies and six half-pennies.*)
DAVE: Sorry I've nothing bigger.
    (LYNDA *sweeps the money off the counter.*)
LYNDA: No bother, we can use the change. Next.
CUSTOMER: I want two cod and fours, a cod and six, a plaice
    and six, two threes, three fours and a couple of sixes, all
    with crispy bits.
LYNDA: Open or closed?
CUSTOMER: Closed.
    (LYNDA *begins to serve the* CUSTOMER, *but watches* DAVE *as
    he gives one of the packets of chips to the young woman.*
    LYNDA *shovels fish and chips into packets.*)
LYNDA: Two cod and four, a cod and six – what else?
CUSTOMER: A plaice and six, two threes, three fours and a
    couple of sixes, all with crispy bits.
LYNDA: Please.
CUSTOMER: Please.

42

47 EXT. THE BACK LANE BY THE MANSELLS' HOUSE.
   DAY
LYNDA *rides slowly up the lane on her bike having just finished
work on the fish and chip van. She has a large portion of chips
wrapped in newspaper. She opens the back gate, pushes the bike in
and leans it against the shed. She thinks for a moment, then goes into
the shed.* MARGARET *is standing in the garden, she is practising
holding the troop flag.*

48 INT. THE SHED. DAY
*The shed is full of junk, a pram, garden tools, etc., accumulated
over years. The Mickey Mouse gas mask hangs on a hook.* LYNDA
looks round the shed. MARGARET *comes to the door and stares at
her.*
LYNDA: Cock off.

49 INT./EXT. BUS GARAGE. EARLY EVENING
DAVE *walks out of the office. He sees* LYNDA *walking towards him
down the centre of the garage. They meet in the middle. He smiles.*
DAVE: Hello, Lynda.
LYNDA: There, you bugger, that's for you.
   (*She shoves the extra large portion of cold vinegar-soaked chips
   into* DAVE's *face and walks off.*)
DAVE: Lynda, I'm sorry.
LYNDA: Too bloody late.

50 INT./EXT. THE MANSELLS' HOUSE: BEDROOM/
   GARDEN. NIGHT
Everything is quiet and still. LYNDA *looks out of her bedroom
window, down the garden and towards the gate, all clearly visible in
the moonlight.* LYNDA *is in her nightdress. She is getting tired. She
yawns then reacts, almost startled. Down by the gate, a figure steps
out of the shadows and stands by the gate. It is* ERIC. *He is smoking
a cigarette. He looks up at Lynda's window.* LYNDA *puts on her
dressing-gown and silently opens her bedroom door.*

43

51 INT. THE MANSELLS' HOUSE: HALL/STAIRS. NIGHT
LYNDA *creeps out on to the landing. She listens at her father's
bedroom door and is surprised to hear muffled laughter. She listens
hard. She hears her father's voice and then the voice of a woman.
She reflects on this minor revelation. Then she makes her way down
the stairs, the stairs creaking and making too much noise as she goes.*

52 EXT. THE MANSELLS' GARDEN. NIGHT
LYNDA *opens the back door and tiptoes her way down the garden
path towards* ERIC.
LYNDA: (*Whispers*) Hello.
   (ERIC *takes a pull on his cigarette, stares at* LYNDA.)
   It's me, the troublesome bugger, remember?
ERIC: About bloody time.
LYNDA: Cheeky sod. What you hanging about here for?
ERIC: Collecting bets.
   (ERIC *stubs out his cigarette, clicks open the gate.*)
   Come stand over by the wall.
LYNDA: Shh. This way. (*Points to the shed.*) Mrs Hartley
   Fartley. Sleeps with one lug out the window. Here. Come on.
   (LYNDA *goes into the shed.*)

53 INT. THE MANSELLS' SHED. NIGHT
LYNDA: Come on, hurry up.
   (ERIC *comes into the shed.* LYNDA *closes the door.*)
   Have you got a match?
   (ERIC *taps his pocket, removes a box of matches and chucks
   them to* LYNDA. LYNDA *strikes a match and lights a candle in
   a holder.*)
   There.
   (ERIC *looks round the shed. It has changed. A space has been
   cleared and, on the floor, there are some pillows and rolled up
   blankets.*)
ERIC: Can I have my matches back?
LYNDA: Mr Mingy.
ERIC: What's this?
   (LYNDA *unrolls the blankets, turning them into a rather cosy
   pallet on the floor.*)

44

LYNDA: There.

ERIC: How many you had on there?
(*This hurts.*)

LYNDA: Oh, a few.

ERIC: How many bus conductors?

LYNDA: Loads. I'm not fussy, that's why I'm here with you.

ERIC: I hear you had a bust-up with your boyfriend.

LYNDA: Word gets round quick, don't it? All the little tongues
go clack, clack, clack.

ERIC: What's all this (*the bedding*) then?

LYNDA: I come here to sleep, to escape my dad and boring
bloody sister.

ERIC: Who with?

LYNDA: You.
(*A beat.* LYNDA *wants* ERIC *to kiss her.* ERIC *unbuttons her
nightdress.*)

ERIC: What have you got in here, then?

LYNDA: Don't know, have to have a look.

ERIC: (*Mimics*) Have a look.
(ERIC *touches her breasts, rather gently, then runs his hand
across her tummy and then down her thighs.*)

LYNDA: (*As he runs his hand up her thigh*) Do you love me?

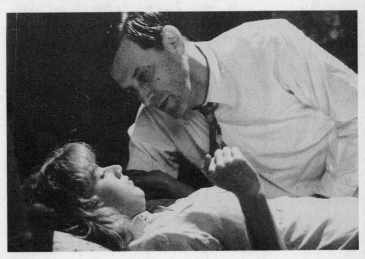

45

ERIC: No. Don't love anybody, not even myself.

LYNDA: Oh, bloody hell. Come on.

> (LYNDA *gets down on the blanket.* ERIC *chucks off his jacket, then struggles with his shoes and trousers.* ERIC *gets down on the floor with* LYNDA.)

ERIC: Think you're it, don't you?

LYNDA: You said that before.

ERIC: Then I must be right.

LYNDA: You don't know how lucky you are, I'm practically a virgin.

> (*They kiss.* ERIC *rolls over on top of* LYNDA.)

LYNDA: You still got your pants on.

ERIC: Not for long.

> (*They kiss again.*)

LYNDA: Take them off.

> (ERIC *begins to take off his underpants.*)

ERIC: No hurry.

> (*They kiss once more, but suddenly break off as, outside, a footstep is heard. They both hold their breath. Silence . . . then another footstep.*)

LYNDA: Oh, God, it's my dad, it's my dad, it's my dad.

ERIC: Quiet.

> (ERIC *blows out the candle. They both lie very still and silent. Another two footsteps.* LYNDA *is terrified, she clings to* ERIC. *The door of the shed clicks open, a sharp intake of breath from* LYNDA *as a piercing bright flashlight hits them both:* LYNDA *with her nightdress up, legs apart;* ERIC *on top of her, in his shirt-tails and socks with his underpants round his knees. A frozen image in the sharp glare of the flashlight.*)

POLICEMAN: (*Very polite*) Oh . . . I beg your pardon, madam.

> (LYNDA's *heart misses a beat.*)

LYNDA: Oh, thank God you're not my father.

> (*The torch goes off.*)

POLICEMAN: I'm very sorry, madam. The gate was open, I thought you might have intruders. Beg y' pardon.

> (*The* POLICEMAN *leaves, shutting the garden gate behind him.* LYNDA *goes to the shed door.*)

LYNDA: Oh my God, bloody hell, if he wakes my father, we're

both dead. I thought it was him, I really did. Listen to my
heart, it's going like a hammer.

(ERIC *lights a cigarette*.)

Shh! Don't light the candle. If he comes out here we're
dead.

ERIC: Come down here and shut up.

LYNDA: Oh, my heart.

(LYNDA *is looking out of the shed window towards the house*.)

ERIC: (*Pulls her down*.) Come here.

(LYNDA *lies beside* ERIC, *listening for any further footsteps*.)

LYNDA: Oh God, I'm shaking like a bag of jelly, can you feel?
We left the bloody gate open.

ERIC: What's the worry? Forget it.

LYNDA: I thought it was him.

ERIC: What's it matter. I can take care of your old man, you
take care of mine.

LYNDA: (*Holding on to* ERIC) Thank God it wasn't him.

ERIC: What's it matter? He don't care.

LYNDA: Who?

ERIC: Your dad. Can't wait to get shot of you. Half a dollar.

LYNDA: (*Staring at* ERIC) That's what you think.

ERIC: That's what I know.

LYNDA: What do you mean?

ERIC: (*Mimics*) What do you mean? He told me. Can't wait to
get rid of you. Thinks you're a bloody nuisance, which you
are. Fed up with looking after you. Big girl like you, should
be looking after yourself. So what if he comes out here, I
don't care.

(*While talking*, ERIC *has been exploring with his hands. A
beat as* LYNDA *absorbs what he has said. She begins to react to
his touch*.)

LYNDA: I can't do it now.

ERIC: Why not?

LYNDA: I'm scared. That copper might come back . . .
(*Laughs*.) . . . bring all the police cadets with him.

ERIC: You're not leaving until you do.

LYNDA: You'll have to wear a plonker.

(ERIC *shakes his head*.)

47

You're not doing it unless you do.

ERIC: You don't know what you're missing.

LYNDA: No plonker, no nooky.

(*Despite what she is saying,* LYNDA *is getting very turned on.
So is* ERIC.)

ERIC: I'm an expert, I know what I'm doing, I'll take care of
you. I'm a cowboy, didn't I tell you that? The best
bareback rider in town.

(LYNDA *says nothing, but it is clear that* ERIC *is going to get
what he wants. Fade in music.*)

54   INT.   BRITISH LEGION HALL.   NIGHT

*The Saturday evening social at the British Legion Ex-Servicemen's
Club is in full swing. A boozy evening. On stage: a piano accordion
and drums duo. At the microphone:* HARRY FIGGIS, *in shirt sleeves,
with a bright red face; and* ERIC, *well tanked up and holding a tin
tray.* HARRY *and* ERIC *are galloping their way through the first
verse of an extremely raucous version of 'Mule Train':* HARRY *sings
the verse. When they get to the chorus,* ERIC *does the shouts and
bullwhip crack by hitting his head with the tin tray. The highspot of
the evening. In the hall, men are in the majority although, being a
social evening, a number of wives and teenage sons and daughters
are present. There are a few men in uniforms, and a young man with
one leg. A preponderance of demob suits, trilby hats and caps. Most
of the men tend to be near the bar, at the other end of the hall from
the stage. Seated at a table close to the stage are:* HUBERT
MANSELL, MARGARET *and* LYNDA. *Also present,* HUBERT's
casual companion, MRS MATHEWS, *cousins* MILLIE *and* JOAN,
and HARRY FIGGIS's *equally large brother,* NEVILLE FIGGIS.
*'Mule Train' comes to a whip-cracking end and it receives an
enthusiastic response. Only Vera Lynn could have gone down bigger.*
ERIC *and* HARRY, *stars for the evening, step down from the stage.
Much whistling and foot stomping from the people.*

MRS MATHEWS: (*Applauding*) That was wonderful! Truly
wonderful. I have to give you a big kiss for that. They
deserve a big kiss. Come here. (*Kisses* ERIC.) You should be
a professional.

48

ERIC: Oh, I am, I am.

MRS MATHEWS: You too, Harry.

   (MRS MATHEWS *kisses* HARRY FIGGIS.)

ERIC: (*Taking advantage*) Any more, any more? What about
   you, Aunt Millie?

MILLIE: Oh, I suppose so, why not?

   (ERIC *kisses* MILLIE.)

   You make me sound like some old woman.

ERIC: You too, Joan.

JOAN: I thought you'd have to have a go at me.

MILLIE: He's not fussy.

   (LYNDA *and* MARGARET *watch this sudden outburst of boozy
   kisses.* MRS MATHEWS *has done* HARRY FIGGIS *and is now
   lunging for* NEVILLE FIGGIS, *saving the biggest one for*
   HUBERT. MRS MATHEWS *breaks out of her clinch with*
   HUBERT, *pats him affectionately on the cheek. He smiles,
   kisses her on the cheek.* MRS MATHEWS *senses* LYNDA *is*

watching her, looks in her direction. LYNDA *is suddenly
shocked to realize there is a relationship between this woman
and her father.*)

ERIC: And the lovely Lynda.

(ERIC *grabs* LYNDA *and kisses her, watched by her father.*)
(*His arm round* LYNDA) Isn't she lovely?
(ERIC's *and* HUBERT's *eyes meet.* HUBERT *shifts his glance to*
LYNDA. ERIC *kisses* LYNDA *and looks back at* HUBERT –)
Lovely!
(– *leaving* HUBERT *in no doubt as to his intentions towards his
daughter. The duo has started to play 'The Hokey-Cokey'.
Everybody takes to the floor and begins to sing, 'You put your
right arm in, your right arm out. In out, etc. . . .' and shaking
it all about.* MARGARET, *somewhat shy and sober, is left
sitting it out.* HUBERT *is in the voluminous clutches of* MRS
MATHEWS *on the one hand and* AUNT MILLIE *on the other.
Knowing that* HUBERT *is watching,* ERIC *kisses* LYNDA *at the
knees-up on the chorus of the 'Hokey-Cokey'.* LYNDA *looks*

51

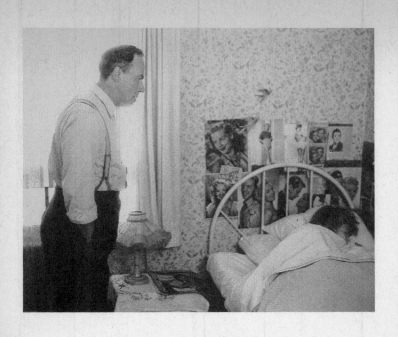

from her father to MRS MATHEWS *and back again. The music carries over into –*)

55 INT./EXT. LYNDA'S BEDROOM/GARDEN. NIGHT
Point of view from Lynda's bedroom of the garden shed illuminated by the moonlight. A warm gentle glow of candlelight from the shed window shows that LYNDA *and* ERIC *are in residence. Music slowly fades. The light in the shed goes out, the shed door opens and* LYNDA *and* ERIC *come out.* LYNDA *is in her nightdress.* ERIC *opens the garden gate, quietly, and closes it behind him.* LYNDA *gives him a quick kiss and tiptoes her way up the garden path.* ERIC *lights a cigarette and walks off down the lane. As* ERIC *disappears from view, the camera moves round to show* HUBERT MANSELL *looking out of the bedroom window.* LYNDA *can be heard creeping her way up the stairs. He does not move.* LYNDA *comes into the bedroom. The presence of her father is totally unexpected.* HUBERT *continues to stare out of the window.* LYNDA *does not move, she's frightened, she waits a few seconds until she recovers. Then, quite*

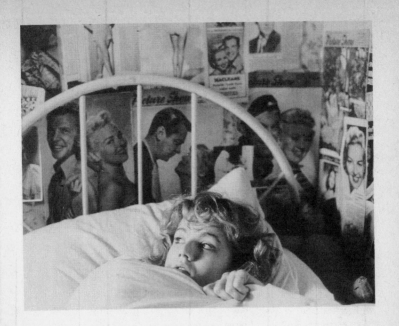

instinctively, she moves towards her bed and gets into it. She lies on
her side, knees up, the covers pulled protectively up under her chin.
HUBERT *stares out of the window.*

HUBERT: (*Quiet*) Your mother wouldn't approve.

LYNDA: Pity she's not here to say.

    (*A moment, this could explode into a venomous row.*)

HUBERT: (*Quiet*) She'd have shown you the door.

LYNDA: I've seen it.

    (*A dangerous moment, venomous anger close to the surface as*
    HUBERT MANSELL *stares at his daughter. The anger subsides,*
    turns sour. He sighs.)

HUBERT: (*Quiet, very matter of fact*) I'm a respected man,
    Lynda. A Freemason. I know that doesn't mean much to
    you. (*Thinks about it.*) Why should it? I'm not here to be
    made a fool of, Lynda. There's such a thing as dignity. You
    seem to think you're smart but I'm afraid you'll end up the
    bloody fool. Just don't do it in my house, that's all. I don't
    want to be witness to that kind of spectacle.

LYNDA: (*From under the covers*) What about Maisie Mathews?
HUBERT: I'm a man. (*Stares at her for some moments.*) I don't
know why you've turned out the way you have. (*Thinks
about it.*) God knows. You're in such a rush. Why be in
such a rush about it all?
(*He goes. The camera moves in on* LYNDA, *curled up in bed,
very still, eyes open.*)

56 INT. MANSELLS' HOUSE: LANDING. DAY
LYNDA *is alone in the house. The landing is empty.* LYNDA *walks
out of her bedroom, across the landing, and into her father's
bedroom.*

57 INT. HUBERT'S BEDROOM. DAY
*On the mantelpiece, there is a photograph of Lynda with her mother
and sister, plus one or two other family pictures and a picture of
Hubert in his Freemason's gear. The room is neat, almost
impersonal, like a ship's cabin.* LYNDA *opens a wardrobe. It is
filled with her father's clothes. At one end, there are three women's
coats and a dress which belonged to her mother. She removes the
dress, touches it, smells it, puts it back. She removes one of the coats,
she knows which one she's looking for, and holds it up to look at it.
Removes the hanger and chucks it in the wardrobe, closes the
wardrobe door and strides out of the bedroom with the coat. Music
begins quietly in the background, a cinema organ playing 'A Reg
Dixon Medley'.*

58 EXT. SEAFRONT: DOME CINEMA/SKATING RINK. DAY
*Above the cinema there is a wooden tower – the dome. On the beach,
there is a ramshackle roller-skating rink with a few coloured bulbs
hung around the perimeter. The 'Reg Dixon Medley' comes out of a
tannoy. Only four customers. Two young women (sixteen or
seventeen). They cannot skate at all, they are clinging to each other,
laughing and screaming hysterically. There is a young man in a
soldier's uniform, he can skate, just a little. And there is a boy
(nine). He skates round and round the rink while the others tumble
about him.* LYNDA *crosses the road towards the cinema and goes into*

*a small entrance next to the main cinema entrance. She is wearing
her mother's coat and carries a suitcase. Above the cinema entrance
is a larger than life cut-out of Betty Grable.*

59 INT./EXT.   THE DOME/SEAFRONT.   DAY
Point of view of the skating rink from a room at the top of the dome.
LYNDA *looks out of the window. Reg Dixon continues. Very little
furniture in this large open room. It's untidy. Sun filters in through
the dusty dirty window. Sound of footsteps on the stairs.* ERIC *stops
when he sees* LYNDA. *He has not expected to see her. He notices the
suitcase on the floor.*
ERIC: (*Taps the suitcase with his foot.*) What's this?
LYNDA: I've left him.
ERIC: Who?
LYNDA: (*Mimics*) Who? Him. And my boring bloody sister. She
   said she wants to join the army. I thought she meant the
   Sally Army but she means the army.
   (*She shakes her head.*)
ERIC: How did you get in?
LYNDA: It's not locked, is it? You said you wanted me through
   the night. Got me now, father's blessing, good riddance.
   (ERIC *takes off his jacket.*)
   I can bugger off if you want.
   (LYNDA *stares out of the window at the roller-skaters.* ERIC
   kicks off his shoes and lies on the bed. He taps LYNDA *on the
   back with his foot.*)
ERIC: Come here.
   (LYNDA *sits on the bed.*)
LYNDA: Cuddle me, please. I'm fed up. I ache inside. I'll clear
   up. It's a bloody mess in here. You stink of booze and fags.
ERIC: You stink of chip fat.
LYNDA: Cod and four, cod and six, two threes, crispy bits, yap,
   yap, yap.
ERIC: (*Sniffs her coat.*) It's this.
LYNDA: No, it's not.
ERIC: Take it off.
   (*Still laying on the bed,* ERIC *helps* LYNDA *to remove her
   coat.*)

55

ERIC: Better take this off an' all. (*Begins to unbutton her dress.*) I
      can just fit you in before the Novices Handicap, Kempton.
      (LYNDA *bursts into tears.*)
      Cor, come on, what's the fuss?
LYNDA: Hold me, please, just hold me.
ERIC: What's the matter? Gone off it, have you? Not going to
      do it any more?
LYNDA: No.
ERIC: Have to ring the papers about this.
LYNDA: I'll go to Bournemouth.
ERIC: You what?
LYNDA: (*Mimics*) You what? Bournemouth. If you don't want
      me I'll go to bloody Bournemouth.
ERIC: (*Still undoing her dress*) I do want you. Don't have fish
      and chip shops in Bournemouth. Or sheds.
      (LYNDA *laughs.*)
      What would you do without fish and chips and sheds and
      my old man?
      (LYNDA *laughs, a mixture of laughter and tears.* ERIC *ploughs
      on with the seduction while, outside on the skating rink, Reg
      Dixon is wading through a 'Spanish Medley'.*)

60   EXT.   THE DOME CINEMA.   DAY
ERIC *walks out of the side entrance of the Dome and away.*

61   INT./EXT.   SKATING RINK/ERIC'S ROOM.   DAY
LYNDA *sits at the end of the bed, partially dressed, staring out of the
window. Tears behind the eyes. The music has stopped. The camera
tracks towards and behind* LYNDA. *For a moment, the sun burns out
the image. The camera continues tracking but the room has changed
to –*

62   INT.   THE MANSELLS' HOUSE.   DAY
It is now Lynda's bedroom and LYNDA, *aged eleven, is sitting on
the bed staring out of the window through which the sun is shining.
It is 1945. Sound of the door being opened.* LYNDA *does not react.*
HUBERT MANSELL *stands in the doorway and looks at his
daughter. He does not know what to do. He could go over to the*

56

*child, to touch her, offer her comfort, but somehow he just can't
make it. He backs out of the room. Standing on the landing behind
him is* AUNT MILLIE. *She comes into the room, takes* LYNDA's
hand.

MILLIE: Come on, lovely.
> (*They walk out of the room on to the landing – just in time to
> see the undertakers carrying Elizabeth Mansell's coffin out of
> the front door. Reverse shot on* LYNDA *and* AUNT MILLIE,
> *holding hands standing at the top of the stairs. Music. Fade in
> a gentle tango played on the piano . . .*)

63   EXT./INT.   PARIS CAFÉ TEA ROOMS.   DAY
Music. LYNDA, VICKIE (*eighteen*) *and* DORIS (*fifty-two*) *pose on
the steps of the Paris Café Tea Rooms. Being the smartest and most
exclusive tea rooms in Bournemouth, they are all dressed in smart
waitress's uniforms: black dress, stockings and shoes with white
apron, hat and frilly collar. Very smart. Also a pencil and order
book hanging from the waist on a length of cord. Holding their trays
high on one hand, they pose for the* SEAFRONT PHOTOGRAPHER,
*turn and walk briskly into the café tea rooms. The Paris Café Tea
Rooms are situated in a large, imposing building. Outside there are
tables on a terrace; the interior is large and imposing with marble
columns and walls. The tables are covered by neat white tablecloths.
The café caters for the most genteel classes who know how to behave
and dress. Day trippers seldom venture inside. As the three waitresses
walk in through the main entrance, the manager walks out to
investigate what they've been up to. He would not approve of
photographers. This man, the manager, bears a striking resemblance
to Joseph Goebbels and holds strict dominion over the tea rooms.*

64   INT.   PARIS CAFÉ TEA ROOMS.   DAY
LYNDA *delivers the order to the waiting table of customers: tea,
sandwiches, scones, etc., served on china plates, teapot, etc.*
LYNDA: Thank you, sir . . . Thank you, modom.
> (*She walks over to take the order of a customer sitting alone at a
> corner table.*)
> Yes, sir.

(*The customer looks up, it is* ERIC. *He is smartly dressed in a new suit.*)

ERIC: Cup of tea, please.

LYNDA: We don't serve cups of tea, sir, only pots. That's teapots, not piss pots, although we can always make exceptions. If you want a cup of tea you must go to a cafe, with all the other riff-raff. This is a café.

ERIC: A pot of tea, then, smart arse.

LYNDA: (*As she turns*) Language.

ERIC: And a bun . . . or a bit of cake.

LYNDA: (*Pen poised for the order*) Bath bun, Chelsea bun, currant bun, honey buns, up your bum, fairy buns, seed cake, cherry cake, fruit cake, ginger cake, Eccles cake, tea cake, lemon cake, swiss rolls, dinkie rolls, jam sandwich, macaroons, cheese straws and scones.

ERIC: I'll just have the tea.

LYNDA: Please.

ERIC: Please.

LYNDA: Thank you.

(LYNDA *heads for the kitchen.*)

65 INT. PARIS CAFÉ KITCHEN. DAY

LYNDA *and* VICKIE *look out of the circular window in the connecting door between the kitchen and the café.*

LYNDA: See that bloke in the corner?

VICKIE: Yeah.

LYNDA: Serve him, will you, Vickie? If he asks where I've gone tell him I've gone to Singabloodypore.

66 INT. PARIS CAFÉ TEA ROOMS. DAY

VICKIE *walks out of the kitchen and serves tea to* ERIC.

VICKIE: Tea, sir.

ERIC: Where's the other young lady?

VICKIE: Pardon?

ERIC: Where's the waitress who took my order?

VICKIE: Oh, you mean the waitress who took your order, sir?

ERIC: That's right.

VICKIE: She's got an urgent call and had to leave, sir.

59

ERIC: Where to?
VICKIE: Singabloodypore, sir.
    (VICKIE *escapes towards the kitchen.*)

67   EXT.   PARIS CAFÉ STAFF ENTRANCE.   EARLY EVENING
LYNDA *and* VICKIE *leave the back entrance to the Paris Café Tea Rooms at the end of their working day. They are both in a good mood,* VICKIE *trips on the step,* LYNDA *grabs her, they both scream and start to giggle as they almost fall over. Then they spot* ERIC *standing in a doorway on the opposite side of the road. This causes hilarity. They walk off down the road whispering and giggling.*
LYNDA: Oh, my God, there he is, there he is. Don't look, don't look, he thinks I've gone to Singabloodypore.
    (*More giggles and laughter. They hold on to each other.*)
    Going to need clean knickers after this.
    (*Another burst of laughter.* VICKIE *trips again, this caused mainly by her high-heeled shoes.*)
VICKIE: Oops!
    (*Hysterical giggles. They attempt to pull themselves together and walk along the road in a sober fashion.* ERIC *follows them.*)

68   EXT.   SEAFRONT.   EARLY EVENING
ERIC *follows* LYNDA *and* VICKIE *along the promenade.* LYNDA *and* VICKIE *giggle, pretending not to notice* ERIC. *They do a little dance.* ERIC *applauds.* LYNDA *suddenly turns on him, violent.*
LYNDA: Why don't you bugger off! Go away! Can't you see when you're not wanted? Don't need none of you. Just bugger off!
ERIC: Lyndie.
LYNDA: Lyndie. Oh, I say, never called me Lyndie before. I bet he's after something. Ha, bloody ha.
    (VICKIE *drifts slightly ahead.* ERIC *trails a pace or two behind* LYNDA.)
ERIC: I miss you. I came to see you.
LYNDA: I bet I know what you're missing.
ERIC: You just cleared off. I come back you'd gone. I thought you'd still be there, I really did.

LYNDA: (*Hesitates.*) Oh . . . just bugger off. I don't want to think about it.

ERIC: What's there to think about? Come on, let's go for a drink.

LYNDA: You're just after your oats.

ERIC: And your friend, I'll take you both for a drink, a meal if you want.

LYNDA: Look out, Vickie, he's after the two of us.

ERIC: I bet you're missing it too.

LYNDA: Do you? How much? How much do you want to bet?

ERIC: I wouldn't want to take your money.

LYNDA: Lynda up the duff then, what odds do you put on that? Eh, Mr Clever Dick?

(ERIC *is suddenly on very uncertain ground.*)

Oh, look, Vickie, that's shut his gob. That's put a crease in his brand new suit.

(*Reaction from* VICKIE *at this piece of news.*)

ERIC: I don't believe you.

LYNDA: Don't you?

(*She walks off.*)

ERIC: You're joking.

LYNDA: Am I?

ERIC: I don't believe you . . . how?

LYNDA: How what?

ERIC: How do you know?

LYNDA: You're the one should know. You put it up me. Mr Bareback Rider. You knew when you were going to spunk, how the hell was I supposed to know?

ERIC: No, you soft cow, I mean how do you know? Are you sure?

LYNDA: You're the one all eyes. Look! (*Shows him her stomach, the smallest bulge.*) Can't you see?

ERIC: No, I can't.

LYNDA: All you see is tits and arses.

ERIC: Have you been to a doctor?

LYNDA: Ha!

(LYNDA *is caught between tears and laughter.*)

ERIC: How do you know it's mine, then?

LYNDA: (*Turns on him.*) If it walks with a limp and thinks it's a
   prick, it's yours!
ERIC: (*Wants to hit back.*) Yeah, but how do you know? I don't
   know that, do I?
LYNDA: You –
   (LYNDA's *temper suddenly goes. A real fight. She attacks*
   ERIC, *tries to smack him round the skull with her handbag.*
   She's out to hurt him, kicking and punching. His hat flies. He
   defends and counter-attacks, tries to smack her around.)
VICKIE: Lynda! Lynda!
   (*A sprawl.* VICKIE *tries to intervene. A mass of arms and legs.*)
Cut to –

69 EXT. ABORTIONIST'S HOUSE. DAY
LYNDA *and* VICKIE *walk down a narrow alley which, quite*
unexpectedly, opens out on to a small, pleasant square. In the
square, there is a small double-fronted house. There is nothing seedy
about this place as the narrow alley might have led us to expect.
LYNDA *and* VICKIE *walk into the square.* VICKIE *refers to her*
piece of paper, points.
VICKIE: (*Almost a whisper*) This is it.
   (LYNDA *stares at the house, at the door, and the bell on the*
   door.)
LYNDA: What does she do, did Winnie say?
VICKIE: No.
LYNDA: Is it knitting needles and all that?
VICKIE: I don't know.
LYNDA: Just think of all those old bags looking down their
   noses. Born with their bloody legs crossed.
VICKIE: It doesn't look too bad.
LYNDA: How much?
   (VICKIE *shows her the piece of paper.*)
   Where am I going to get that sort of money? (*Looks at the*
   door for some moments.) Let's go have a cup of tea.
   (*They leave.*)

70 INT. PARIS CAFÉ TEA ROOMS. DAY
LYNDA *walks quickly out of the kitchen of the Paris Café Tea*
Rooms and sees her father sitting at one of the tables. Instant nerves.

*She serves tea and toasted tea cake to a customer – the café is busy –
she spills some tea on the tablecloth.*

LYNDA: Sorry, madam.

    (*She goes over to her father, pad in hand, ready for the order.*)
    Yes, what do you want?

    (HUBERT *does not reply, just stares at his daughter.*)
    Can I help you, sir?

HUBERT: The moment I saw you walk through that door, I
    thought, that's my daughter and she's a slut.

LYNDA: Thank you, sir, will that be all, sir?

HUBERT: Don't be clever, Lynda, from where I'm sitting you
    don't look clever.

LYNDA: Bath buns, Chelsea buns, currant buns, honey buns,
    plain buns, I know why you're here and I don't want to
    discuss it so do you want a pot of tea or would you prefer to
    just clear off?

HUBERT: I'm disgusted, Lynda.

LYNDA: With lemon, sir?

HUBERT: I thought I could have a perfectly reasonable conversation with you. I thought I could come here –

LYNDA: I don't want you here. I'm at work and I've got Hermann Goebbels breathing down me neck. Just clear off. (*Two women at the next table begin to pick up on the exchange.*)

HUBERT: I thought I could come here and have a reasonable conversation with you but all I want to do now is clout you one.

LYNDA: Would you like a pot of tea first, sir? (*The* MANAGER *is now watching.* HUBERT *is holding in his anger.*)

HUBERT: Listen to you, you and your mouth, look where it's got you.

LYNDA: Dad, I can't discuss it. Will you just go away? I need this job. (*The* MANAGER *is on his way over to the table.*)

HUBERT: You're going to need more than a job.

LYNDA: Dad, please, just bugger off.

MANAGER: Is anything the matter, Miss Mansell? Is everything to your satisfaction, sir?

HUBERT: No, it is not.

LYNDA: (*Mimics.*) Is anything the matter, Miss Mansell? Is everything to your satisfaction, sir?

HUBERT: (*To the* MANAGER) You see? What can you do? How do you put up with it? (*More and more people are becoming aware of the friction.*)

LYNDA: Oh, shut up.

MANAGER: Please. This is disgraceful, go to the kitchen immediately, Miss Mansell.

LYNDA: No, I won't go to the kitchen. Stuff the bloody kitchen.

HUBERT: Just watch your mouth!

MANAGER: Please!

HUBERT: (*To the* MANAGER) This is what you get, you see, this is what it's like, now you can begin to see my side of it.

LYNDA: Oh, please, just bugger off.

MANAGER: Please!

LYNDA: I said please.

HUBERT: You see?

MANAGER: What is going on, what is going on?

HUBERT: I've given a lot of time –

MANAGER: Please, sir.

HUBERT: – made a lot of sacrifices –

LYNDA: Oh God.

HUBERT: – though, God knows, you wouldn't think it.

LYNDA: (*To a* CUSTOMER) What are you staring at, you old bag?

(*Shock horror from the* CUSTOMER.)

MANAGER: (*To* LYNDA) Please! (*To the* CUSTOMER) Mrs ... Madam ... please!

LYNDA: Well, she is an old bag –

MANAGER: That is enough!

HUBERT: Lynda!

MANAGER: (*To the* CUSTOMER) Please accept my apologies, this is disgraceful, quite unprecedented.

LYNDA: (*Through the above*) She comes in here every day, she does, she whinges about everything.

MANAGER: (*To the* CUSTOMER) I have been at the Paris Café Tea Rooms since the end of the war and before that –

LYNDA: (*Through the above*) Yap, yap, yap, every bloody day.

MANAGER: (*To* LYNDA) That is enough. Language, please!

LYNDA: It's true. What's wrong with the truth?

MANAGER: You're fired, you are dismissed, get out.

(*Everybody is now watching, the café is at a standstill.*)

LYNDA: (*To everybody, about the* MANAGER) This one goes around with his brown nose, up in the air, down on the carpet, lardy-dah this, lardy-dah that. (*Announces*) The cook spits in the buns and we all piss in the teapots.

(*A customer holds her mouth, another customer chokes on her tea.*)

MANAGER: Out! Ladies and gentlemen –

HUBERT: She's a bad lot, that's the truth, nothing but trouble. That's the way it's always been.

LYNDA: This is my father.

HUBERT: (*Gives testimony*) Ever since she could speak she's uttered nothing but filth. From the day she uttered her first word. Her tongue has caused nothing but trouble.

66

LYNDA: This is my father speaking.

HUBERT: Sometimes I doubt it.

LYNDA: An insult to my dead mother.

MANAGER: (*Who has gone very pale*) I'm sorry, but this cannot go on.

LYNDA: I'm up the duff! That's what's up his nose. I'm pregnant. In the club!
(*Shock horror.*)

MANAGER: Right! That's it! That's enough.

LYNDA: A man's willy has entered my person and left a little visitor behind.
(*More shock horror. The* MANAGER *marches purposefully in one direction, then the other, like a chicken with no head.*
LYNDA *is by now standing on a chair.*)

HUBERT: Get down.

MANAGER: This is a matter for the police. Ladies and

67

gentlemen, ladies and gentlemen, please remain calm. I am calling the police.

(LYNDA *climbs on to the table as the* MANAGER *retreats to the kitchen where he watches from behind the protection of the kitchen door. He does not call the police.*)

LYNDA: (*Points to* HUBERT.) This is my father. This is the man who once gave one to Gracie Fields.

HUBERT: Down.

LYNDA: A Freemason, a member of the British Legion.

HUBERT: Get down!

LYNDA: Am I the only one who does it?

HUBERT: This is not my daughter!

LYNDA: What do you lot do? Eh?

HUBERT: (*With passion*) This is not my daughter! Not my daughter!

LYNDA: What do you lot play with in bed at night? Eh?
(*Total shock horror.*)

HUBERT: I disown her!

LYNDA: Hands up all those who like willies. I do.
(*The* MANAGER *bursts out of the kitchen with the* COOK.)

MANAGER: The police are coming.

LYNDA: Balls!

HUBERT: Ladies and gentlemen, I would like to apologize for this disgraceful display.

LYNDA: So what, I'm up the duff, who cares?

HUBERT: Please continue with your teas.

LYNDA: I like willies.

HUBERT: I will settle. (*To the* MANAGER) All these teas on me, all right?

MANAGER: Get her down.

LYNDA: You all look as if you could do with a bit. Sex! All of you. All you old bags look as if you could do with a nice bit of *hot willy*!

MANAGER: Get her down!

LYNDA: Sex!
(*The* MANAGER, HUBERT, *the* COOK *and the* MAGISTRATE *all grab* LYNDA. *They come crashing down across the tables causing total chaos. The men appear to sustain severe hernias.*)

68

LYNDA *crawls out from under the table unscathed. She walks smartly towards and out of the kitchen door, to the applause of* VICKIE, DORIS *and the other waitresses.*)

71 INT. CINEMA. DAY
A large and virtually deserted cinema. The camera moves towards a lone figure seated in the centre of the cinema. LYNDA, *still wearing her mother's coat, sits sad, dejected and lonely. The sound of the movie continues: Barbara Hutton sings 'It had to be you' from 'The Beautiful Blonde from Bashful Bend'. Music over into –*

72 EXT. PROMENADE. DAY
LYNDA *meets* AUNT MILLIE *outside a café on the promenade.*
MILLIE: Hello, Lyndie.
LYNDA: Hello, Aunt Millie.
    (*They embrace, both of them almost cry.*)

MILLIE: Thought I'd come and see you. What shall we do?

LYNDA: I could murder a bun and a cup of tea.

MILLIE: So could I. Come on, let's go.

(LYNDA *puts her arm through* MILLIE'*s arm and hugs her as they walk into the café.*)

73 INT./EXT. CAFÉ. DAY

Being the arse-end of the season, there are very few people around. LYNDA *and* MILLIE *sit at a window seat drinking tea and eating buns. Immediately outside the window is the beach and the sea. Late afternoon, the sun shines across the sea into the café.*

MILLIE: How long is it now?

LYNDA: Three months, more or less.

MILLIE: So it's not too late.

LYNDA: ... No.

MILLIE: What happened?

LYNDA: When?

MILLIE: Your father came home very sorry for himself, whatever happened?

(LYNDA *thinks about it, begins to laugh.*)

LYNDA: Silly bugger. I stood up on a chair, in the Paris Tea Rooms, and shouted. Can't remember what I said. It was terrible.

(MILLIE *is amused.*)

He offered to pay for everybody's teas.

(*She laughs.*)

MILLIE: You didn't need to do that, not to your father.

LYNDA: I'm not coming back, you know, no matter what.

MILLIE: What are you going to do then? What chance have you got on your own with a baby? Where are you going to live?

LYNDA: Not in that dump.

MILLIE: Nobody's asking you to, my dear. (*Laughs.*) Things like this don't happen in that kind of town. I can just see your father's face.

LYNDA: Go down well at the Freemasons.

(MILLIE *laughs.*)

MILLIE: He didn't have to stick with you, you know, when your mum died. Or your sister.

70

LYNDA: My boring bloody sister.

MILLIE: You leave her alone, she's all right. Thank God she's not like you. Two of you like that, my God. He could have put you in a home, you know, not many men would have done what he did. On his own with two young girls.

(LYNDA *might cry*.)

LYNDA: He didn't love me.

MILLIE: Oh, yes he did.

LYNDA: Didn't show it.

MILLIE: Can't show that kind thing, not in this day and age. (*A beat*.) You're a pretty young thing, you're funny, but you're pretty. You could get yourself a nice husband, somebody to really look after you.

LYNDA: Do you think?

MILLIE: Yes, I do. But not like that. Who's going to want you like that? It's not too late. Not yet. Do you know where to go if you wanted to get rid of it?

LYNDA: It's all right for you to say that, it's not you that has to do it.

MILLIE: No. That's right, Lyndie, you're right.

LYNDA: What if I had it?

MILLIE: Then have it adopted.

(*This suggestion hurts* LYNDA *more than the idea of an abortion*.) You must have thought about it. Keep that kid, nobody will want you, nobody will want to know you, nobody will want to own you. Nobody. Forget the whole thing, bury it, that's my advice, nobody needs to know a thing about it. Christ, it's tough enough you don't have to go around banging your head with a hammer. Look at me, look at your father. I'm hardly ancient, nor is he. I lost Bill, he lost your mother, and we're on our own. Stuck. There's always enough pain.

LYNDA: What about Maisie Mathews?

MILLIE: And why shouldn't he? What do you expect him to do the rest of his life? I wish I had somebody.

LYNDA: I hope he used a plonker. I'd hate to see what come out of her.

(MILLIE *laughs*.)

71

MILLIE: That's good advice coming from you.
> (*She watches* LYNDA. LYNDA's *eyes fill with tears.*)

LYNDA: Sunday School. Feels just like bloody Sunday School.

MILLIE: You've got to make your own mind up. I've got to go.

LYNDA: Not yet.

MILLIE: It's the buses. I stood around hours waiting for you.

LYNDA: I'm sorry.
> (MILLIE *is fiddling around with her handbag.*)

MILLIE: Here. (*Takes an envelope from her bag.*) Think about what I said. You've got to look after yourself, Lyndie. Here.
> (*She slides the envelope across the table to* LYNDA.)

Would you know where to go, if that's what you decided?

LYNDA: (*Tears falling on the table*) To get rid of it?

MILLIE: If that's what you decided.

LYNDA: I could find out.
> (MILLIE *stands.*)

MILLIE: I'm going to go so just you take care.
> (MILLIE *quickly kisses* LYNDA *on the forehead and leaves the café.* LYNDA *remains sitting at the table.* MILLIE *walks out of the café, past where* LYNDA *is sitting on the other side of the window. They do not look at each other. The envelope is rather old and crumpled. It is not sealed.* LYNDA *touches it for the first time, one finger inside the envelope to look at the money within. She remains sitting in the café.*)

74 EXT. THE PROMENADE. DAY

LYNDA, *wearing her mother's coat, walks along the seafront. High tide. A young woman (sixteen) rides past her on a bike.*

75 EXT. ABORTIONIST'S HOUSE. DAY

LYNDA *walks along the narrow alley and into the square. She stops outside the small double-fronted house. The front door is slightly open. Music from a wind-up gramophone, Mozart's* Così fan tutte, *comes from within the house.* LYNDA *stands at the half-open door.*

76 EXT. BUS STATION. DAY
A single-decker Green Line bus turns into the Southern Automated
Bus Company Station, watched by INSPECTOR HARRY FIGGIS.
As the bus passes, LYNDA *can be seen sitting on the bus.* HARRY
watches LYNDA *as she stares impassively out of the window. The*
bus stops, the door opens, the passengers begin to alight. LYNDA *is*
the last to get off. She is wearing a bright yellow dress. HARRY
FIGGIS *spies round the end of the bus. He watches as* LYNDA *turns*
towards the bus door and an unseen helping hand passes down
LYNDA's *baby to her. She puts the baby into the pram and tucks it*
in. Music. A grand march played on a large cinema organ. LYNDA
begins her Big Parade.
Cut to –

77 INT. BUS GARAGE. DAY
Music continues. LYNDA *marches into the garage pushing the baby*
in the pram soon attracting the attention of DAVE *and other bus*
conductors. LYNDA *marches in one door, across the wide expanse of*
the garage, and out the other side, never looking back.
And cut to –

78 EXT. HAIRDRESSER'S. DAY
LYNDA *and baby in the pram march past her father's shop. The*
shop is closed. On she goes.

79 EXT. SEAFRONT. DAY
The promenade. A group of youths, almost identical to that seen
earlier, are hanging around on the promenade. BRIAN *is among*
them. LYNDA *has now built up a momentum. She marches along the*
promenade towards the youths, cutting a path through the middle of
the group.
LYNDA: Hello. Hello, Brian. Hello, you lot.
   (*The youths fall silent as they watch* LYNDA *walk off along the*
   promenade. LYNDA *looks back over her shoulder, smiles and*
   wiggles her bum as –)
Cut to –

80 EXT. RECREATION GROUND. DAY
The crown green bowlers are out in force. ERIC *is there, on his usual*
patch, collecting bets. LYNDA *pushes the pram across the recreation*

ground and out on to the bowling green. Slowly, one by one, all the heads turn and watch LYNDA. LYNDA *smiles as she passes the* GROUNDSMAN.

LYNDA: (*Quite loud, to the* GROUNDSMAN) Yes, it's mine.

    (*Everybody just stares.* LYNDA *sees* ERIC, *but ignores him.*)

LYNDA: (*To herself*) All mine.

81 EXT. STREET. DAY

LYNDA *and baby turn the corner and head up the street towards her father's house. They stop at the house.* LYNDA *knocks on the front door. She leans forwards into the pram and takes out the baby. All smiles, she lifts the baby high above her head into the air. She holds it in the air for some moments, then brings it down and kisses it, just as the front door begins to open.*

Mix to – Image of LYNDA *riding her bike set against the sky, which mixes to:*

The ELDERLY LADY *on the painted box tap dances and mimes to 'Lost in a Dream' played on the wind-up gramophone.*